Sweet Dreams, Little One – Part 1

A DDLG and MDLG Story About Emma, an ABDL Who Fell Into Mommy and Daddy's Arms Just at the Right Time

By Tina Moore

Table of Contents

Chapter 1

The sound of the tile cutter matched that of an industrial wood chipper, and Emma did her best to block the noise out as she ran down the hallway towards the kitchen.

Why are they cutting the tiles? She asked herself.

They know I need to give the final measurements before they start, she said to herself as she covered her ears. Emma rushed through the opening that was once the kitchen door. Her messy, wavy hair made her look more like an artist than a carpenter. The men who made up her crew were busy at work, installing the kitchen for their clients. Tim, their electrician, stood at the top of his ladder, putting in the new energy-efficient lights. Builder Alex was installing door handles onto a cupboard, but tiler Mark was the culprit operating the tile cutter. They all paused and stared at Emma the moment she burst through the door.

"What are you doing!?" Her exasperated

voice was high pitched as she spoke. "We need the final approval before you can start cutting the tiles. You can't just whip out the cutter and go ahead without the green light from the clients." Her crew had a habit of doing this sort of thing. It wasn't that they were rushing the job. They didn't consider that a client's mind could change from one minute to the next, and without double-checking, materials had the potential to be wasted.

"What are you stressing about, Em?" Mark laughed at her crazed look.

"They marked where they wanted the tiles, so that's where we're putting them," he added.

"Relax, Em. You stress too much," Tim chirped as he climbed down from the ladder. He wrapped one arm around her shoulder and pulled her in close as he said, "All this stress is starting to age you. We can barely tell that you're 40 anymore." Mark and Alex burst into laughter. Emma elbowed Tim in the chest and pushed him away while holding back a smile.

"I'm 27, you idiot!" Her laughter spilled out as she spoke. "You should still wait for me before you start cutting. We don't want to mess this up. These guys are big clients."

"Every client is a big client!" Alex said as he rolled his eyes. "It's not like anyone other than the rich and famous can afford to replace an entire kitchen with the materials that we use!"

"Keep your voice down," Emma hushed her voice, hoping her crew would copy her. She turned back toward Mark, the look on her face making him pause.

"Don't screw this up for us, Mark. Your disdain for the rich and famous is written all over your face whenever you see a client," Emma added.

"The rich and famous may not tickle your fancy, but at least they pay your bills," Tim agreed with Emma.

"Whatever! Can I get back to cutting now, Em, or do you want to double-check those *people* again?" Emma grunted. She hated it when they called her Em instead of her full name.

"You can finish putting the doors back on their hinges, while I go upstairs and ask the clients to finalize the tile placements. Got it?" Emma was firm when she spoke. Emma left the crew and made her way back to the clients. She was sure to fix her hair and calm herself down before knocking on the door.

Emma hated talking to clients. It was the worst part of the job for her. She never felt good enough to be respected as their equal, merely a servant, completing a job. Sure, they were never outwardly rude, but the energy of the dynamic was not one she enjoyed experiencing. She would prefer to be in the kitchen with the guys, finalizing the kitchen's style and build. Alex was right about the clients. They were all rich, and most of the time, they were stuck up and demanded respect that they didn't earn, but Tim was also right. Their cash paid the bills.

She got the information she needed and got back

to work. They finalized the measurements for the tiles, and Mark went back to cutting. She instructed Mark on the style of the tile placement before asking Alex to help her with the doors. The kitchen was coming together. They should be finished with it by the end of the day. Emma prided herself on the ability to run a tight ship.

"Are we going for drinks later?" Tim asked the crew as they packed their equipment into the back of the company truck.

"I'm in!" Alex yelled from the front of the house.

"Sure, but I'm probably driving, so I'll only have a few. What about you, Em, you going to join us this time?" Mark replied, looking directly at Emma. Emma looked up from her tablet and shook her head before promptly returning to her work. She liked to keep up to date with every invoice to make sure everything was listed and charged accordingly.

"Come on, Em! You skip out on the fun stuff all the time," Alex nudged her in the side.

"You're turning into an old lady. Soon the only birthday gifts we'll be getting you is cat food."

"I'm allergic to cats," Emma mumbled. "I don't have the time tonight, guys. I need to run some numbers, so I can make sure we each get our cut."

"We're not going to bug you about our pay, Em. You can take the night off and work on the numbers tomorrow," Tim insisted. Emma looked up from her screen one more time to see the guys staring at her. Their wide eyes resembled that of a puppy begging for a treat. She gave them her best grin but shook her head, "I can't come tonight, guys, maybe next time."

"That's what you always say," Alex muttered under his breath just before he closed the door.

"See you tomorrow," Tim patted her on the shoulder before climbing into the back of the truck. Emma waved them off as they drove away. She hated disappointing them but drinking at the bar all night just wasn't her idea of a good time. She had other plans.

When Emma finally got home, she fell straight into her usual nightly routine. She undressed and drew a bath. She cleaned herself properly and made sure to throw her dirty clothes into the wash. She smiled to herself as she took out a diaper and onesie, running her fingers over the material before dressing herself and instantly feeling at peace. She made herself some eggs and bacon for dinner and carefully cleaned up after herself. When she was done eating, she put her dishes in the dishwasher, went through the house, and made sure all of her chores were done before sitting down to her laptop.

Emma glanced at the photo on her desk of the night she, Mark, Alex, and Tim went to Disneyland for her birthday. It was hard for her to keep her secret from them, but she knew they wouldn't understand. She sighed at the picture as she turned on her laptop and logged onto a site called *The Play Area*. She found it a couple of months ago and spent as much time as possible there. This is what she had been looking forward to all day. This is how she spent her evenings searching for a Mommy and Daddy. Her laptop pinged with a message, and she was quick to open it up. The message was from a user called Daddy-Knows-Best. Emma had been chatting to this guy for a few months, and her eyes shone, and her cheeks glowed as she read the words he had sent.

Hey there, little one, have you finished all of your chores today?

Emma typed quickly, she was going to ask him something tonight, and she didn't want to give herself an excuse to talk herself out of it.

Yes, Daddy, I did all of my chores.

That's good! Did you eat all of your food and clean between your toes in the bath?

Yes, Daddy, I even washed my dishes when I finished eating. I was a very good girl today. Emma beamed as she typed. Daddy-Knows-Best is her favorite out of all the

Mommies and Daddies she'd spoken to online. He was the only online play partner who seemed like he was willing to commit to her, and tonight she planned on asking him the big question.

You've been a perfect girl. What do you want your reward to be?
Emma took a deep breath as she dragged her fingers slowly across the keyboard. She typed out the question and second-guessed it immediately. Yet she needed to ask him. She'd waited long enough and now wanted something more out of this relationship.

I want to see you, Daddy. She pressed send and waited. There was no reply.

I want to see you in person, please. She added. There was still no reply. Emma leaned back and picked at the skin next to her thumbnail as her stomach began to tie in knots. Her computer was silent, and there was no sign of a reply. He didn't usually take this long to answer.

"I shouldn't have asked," she muttered to

herself. "It's too soon. What was I thinking?" She nearly jumped out of her skin when her laptop pinged, and she jerked the mouse to open the reply.

I'm not sure that's a good idea, little one. I think what we have going now is a good thing, and we shouldn't rush things. You've been a really good girl lately, but we should go for smaller rewards. How about we video chat? Would that make you happy?

Emma read the message over and over again, and she didn't know what to think. Her heart was in her stomach, and a lump was forming in her throat. Something told her that it would always be too soon. She took a deep breath and placed her hands on the keyboard. She didn't know what to say, but she let her heart control her fingers and pressed send.

I don't want to video chat right now, Daddy. I missed my nap earlier, so I should go to bed early tonight. Can we talk tomorrow?

Emma found herself biting the bottom of her lip

and stopped. She needed to get control of these bad habits of hers. Her thoughts were tangled up when she glanced down and read the reply.

That's not good! You shouldn't skip your nap. Okay, get some sleep, and we'll talk more tomorrow.

Emma clicked to go offline and closed her laptop. She sat, perfectly still and completely silent, for a long time. Her subtle short breaths echoed in the empty one-bedroom studio apartment. She looked around and wondered how she let herself get like this. She can't keep chasing after Daddies and Mommies online who don't want to commit to her. She needed someone willing to go all-in like she wanted to do.

"Why," she whispered. "Why can't I find a Mommy or Daddy who wants to meet up with me?" She put the laptop back on the table and tried to sleep, but she didn't feel like sleeping. So she stayed up later than she usually did and ran the numbers for the last job. As the hours ticked by, Emma was surprised by how quiet it was, not

just in her apartment, but out on the street. The
only sound she could hear was her heartbeat
echoing through the rooms, and the buzz of the
fridge. Through the silence of the night, one last
sound echoed out. Emma's head snapped back at
the table where her laptop sat. She was frozen for
a fraction of a second as she thought about who
had messaged. Could it be her Daddy changing
his mind and agreeing to meet her? She rushed
over to her laptop. Her hopes were high, and her
smile was wide.

She flipped the lid open and scanned the
notifications for the one she wanted, but she
didn't find it. It was an email that made her
laptop light up in the night. She briefly glanced
at the name from the email, but it was about
work, so she didn't need to deal with it at that
exact moment. Sadly, she put her laptop away
and headed to bed. The night seemed even
quieter now, and her heart felt heavier than it did
before.

Chapter 2

The next day Emma headed into work early, as usual, and planned to look over her emails and messages once she got there. She was always in the office first. Emma enjoyed the quiet time in the morning to drink her coffee and get things in order.

When she arrived, she was surprised to see a car already waiting outside. It was the type of car she was used to seeing her client's drive, but rarely had she had clients who turned up unannounced at her office and never before opening hours. After fumbling with the strap on her laptop bag, she got out of her car and headed towards the office. She glanced at the car as she passed it. Emma couldn't see through the tinted windows, so she kept walking, quickening her pace. She struggled with her mass of keys, looking for the one that fit the front door. She heard the car doors open behind her, and she hurried to find the right key. Footsteps strolled towards her as she dropped the keys to the floor. Emma dashed down to pick them up and jammed the right one into the door just as the footsteps stopped behind her.

"Excuse me, are you Emma by any chance?" The voice behind her was soft and smooth as silk. She thought the woman must be as beautiful as she sounded.

"We emailed you last night about having a kitchen installed," a second voice said, heavy and deep. It carried weight as if the owner was strong and powerful. Emma turned slowly to face the voices, leaving her keys hanging from the still locked door. She looked up at the most beautiful set of people she'd ever seen. They towered over her in a nonthreatening way. The shadow they cast was warm and protective. Emma felt comfortable immediately and had to force herself from entering her little space. Her mind ran wild, trying to remember the name she saw as she glanced over the email last night. The email she didn't open. She wished now that she had taken the time to read it.

"Oh, are you Nora?" she asked carefully. She was prepared to wince if she got it wrong.

"Yes, that's me," the woman replied, her eyes smiling. "You did get our email then. I'm so glad. I was worried because we sent it quite late." Emma eyed the couple suspiciously, but something about them created a magnetic pull.

"No, it wasn't too late," Emma assured her. "I saw it just before I went to bed, but unfortunately, I didn't have the time to read it fully."

"That's alright. We can talk about it now if you've got time," the man replied rather than asked as he gently brushed, passed Emma. He stretched out his arm to unlock the door. "After you." Emma glanced at the open door and back at them. She shot them a weak grin before walking through the door. She rolled her eyes when her back was turned to them.

Typical rich people thinking that all I do is wait around to be summoned by them, Emma thought, annoyed that this guy just assumed that she had nothing else to do that morning. It wasn't that he was wrong, Emma didn't have a kitchen to install that day and had planned to do paperwork, but it was the assumption that irritated her. They followed after her, and the man closed the door behind them before handing her the keys.

"Please, have a seat," Emma said, as she gestured to the two free seats in front of her desk as she sat in hers. The couple glanced around the room one last time before sitting down. Emma could tell by their faces that they approved of the office space and smiled to herself, surprised that she had wanted their approval.

"What can I help you with today?" Emma asked them.

"My husband Jackson and I were hoping to get a new kitchen installed," Nora explained. Emma had to force herself to listen to Nora as she found herself entranced by Nora's seductive voice.

"We saw some pictures of kitchens that you've previously installed, and love your style, and craftwomanship," Nora added, placing her hand on Jackson's thigh.

"She can't stop talking about that marble counter you did with the wooden overlay section. She loves it," the man, who Emma now knew to be Jackson, added.

"Listen, when Nora wants something, she gets it, and she wants a kitchen designed by you," Jackson added, making Emma laugh.

"Well, I am more than happy to help create your dream design," Emma beamed.

"When were you looking to have the kitchen installed?" Emma said, turning her computer screen around so they could see when she was available for them.

"As soon as possible," Nora said, noticing that Emma had a free day today.

"There was a problem with the pipes in our home, and now the entire kitchen has water damage," Jackson explained further. It was clear from his expression that he was unimpressed by the situation, and Emma could only imagine that after paying what she assumed to be millions for the property, that she would be equally as annoyed if it were her home.

Emma had to continually stop herself from gazing like a star-struck fool at Nora and Jackson's beauty. Nora's dark brown, long hair contrasted Jackson's short, wavy hair. Hers bounced and waved with movement while his hair was styled and stayed put. They were both taller than Emma, but Jackson's long neck and broad shoulders made Nora's tall body look tiny. Emma couldn't help but notice that her panties were getting wet, and she raised an eyebrow to herself, trying to get her mind under control. Emma shook her head to clear the thought and focus on her work.

"Okay, so this is how the process goes. We need to make a time to come to look at the space and do an initial measure of what we are working with. Then you can choose to come back here to select your materials and finishes, or I can bring everything to you, whatever works best. After that, it's just a matter of playing around with the space we have. We have a program that shows your space and design selections in 3D to make any final changes more visual. Then I'll do a final measure, and everything gets sent off to manufacturing. Once the design is ready, we can pick a date and start gutting the old kitchen and installing the new one. Depending on the design process, the whole thing from now till finish could take three months, longer if there are lots of changes," she explained as professionally as she could.

"Good, let's book a time for the initial measure then. Can you bring your material samples on the same day? I want to do that all in one go," Nora said, taking Emma by surprise. Emma paused for a moment and looked to Jackson for confirmation. It was clear that Nora got whatever it was that she wanted, but Jackson made the final call. The corner of his lips lifted slightly, and he nodded his head.

"Absolutely," Emma.

"Are you free today? I want to get this started," Nora asked. Emma smiled, pretending to look over her schedule.

"Yes, does 1 pm work for you?" Emma asked. She looked at Jackson as he stood up and began to walk to the door.

"That sounds perfect, Emma. See you soon," Nora said, standing up and walking with Emma to the door. Emma liked that the couple didn't waste any time. They saw what they wanted, and they took no time to get it. Emma opened the door for them, just as Nora took Emma's wrist and pulled her in for a hug and squeezing her tight and taking Emma by surprise. Emma's eyes widened as Nora's arms wrapped around her, but she didn't fight it. The hug felt soft and comforting, and Emma smiled as she felt Nora's breasts against her own. Emma wanted to fall into it further, but she made sure to stay professional. Jackson nodded to her as he wrapped his arm around his wife and walked her to their car, and Emma walked back into the office, hoping that Nora and Jackson didn't notice her blushing cheeks.

"Isn't she just the cutest?" Nora gasped as they drove home. Nora knew that she would be thinking about Emma for hours to come. Jackson gave a slight nod of agreement and grunt as he turned the corner as he pulled into their gated drive-way.

"She's adorable," he replied, knowing that just like himself, his wife would want more than just a new kitchen and hug from Emma.

***

Emma had spent the last two months going over Nora and Jackson's designs and material selection. Between Nora's flirty ways and Jackson's alluring mystery, Emma often spent the evening following one of their meetings pleasuring herself to sleep. She had longed for the day to have constant time with them, and as they booked a date to begin the kitchen demolition, Emma could hardly wait.

On the morning of the demolition, she paced back and forth as she waited for her crew to arrive. She rechecked the time and called all of them for the second time. Her breathing was heavy, and her heart slammed against her chest as she dialed Tim's number.

"Tim!" She cried out as soon as he picked up. "Why the hell did it take you so long to answer? You guys need to get to the office right now! We are gutting that kitchen today for the movie producer clients. I can't get through to Alex or Mark. Can you call them and get down here now." Even though Tim was their electrician, he still helped with the demolition phase of a remodel. Emma had thought it was strange when she had begun working with them but soon learned that the three were almost inseparable. Plus, it made the job quicker, so she continued to allow it.

"Uh…" Tim's voice was slow, and he paused to burp. Emma winced at the sound. "I don't think I can come in today…I may have drunk too much last night," he stammered.

"You have got to be kidding me!" Emma grunted, and she had to stop herself from throwing the phone across the room.

"I seriously can't come in today. Sorry Em. Call Alex and Mark. I don't think they drank as much as me last night," he replied.
Emma let out a long, loud grunt and hung up the phone. She quickly dialed both Mark and Alex, but they gave her the same excuse.

"How could you be hungover?" Emma yelled at Mark through the phone. "You were driving last night!"

"We walked home," Alex said, squinting as he did so, knowing that they had let Emma down and feeling terrible for it. She rolled her eyes, knowing that she would be getting her revenge at some point in the future and hung up the phone, collapsing dramatically into her chair. Her computer pinged as the email came through from Nora.

Emma sighed and stood up. Her face was rock hard, and her eyes squinted. She had to do this on her own. She couldn't let this opportunity pass because her coworkers decided to get drunk on a work night.

"Let's go!" She whispered to herself as she grabbed the keys for the truck and headed out of the door.

Chapter 3

Emma hadn't been surprised to find herself driving into one of the most expensive neighborhoods in the city. The house stood tall on a large estate surrounded by perfectly trimmed hedges and tamed trees. The grass was lush, green, and mowed daily. Sprinklers turned on periodically in each corner of the garden. Their house was only different from the others in the neighborhood by its mansion appearance. Emma drove the company truck down the cobblestone driveway, around a large water fountain placed in the center of the front garden, and parked right at the front of the house. She admired the fountain and wished she could have a miniature one on her table at home. It had fish carved out of marble branching out from the center column, on top of which sat a beautiful mermaid braiding her hair over her shoulder. She didn't spend too much time admiring the place. She was here to do a job. She hoped she could create a kitchen that could live up to the beauty and status of the rest of the house.

"Emma!" Nora ran down the stairs and threw her arms around her. "I'm so glad you could make it. Where's your crew?"

"Oh, they're..." Emma paused and glanced back at the empty truck she drove. She couldn't tell them the guys were hungover. So instead, she opted for, "They have the flu. I called them this morning, and somehow they all just caught the flu. They hang out a lot at the same bars, so maybe they got it from someone there."

"That's unfortunate," Jackson spoke calmly and mysteriously as he walked down the stairs to join Emma and Nora at the bottom.

"Should we reschedule?" He eyed her, making her question herself.

"No. It might take a day or so longer, but I can do it," Emma explained.

"Oh, that's wonderful," Nora grabbed Emma's hand and led her through their home. Emma looked around the space and stifled her sigh as she exhaled.

This might have been a bigger job than I first thought, she thought to herself as she placed her tools on the ground.

"You didn't want any of this saved, did you?" Emma asked Nora, who just shook her head.

"Great, well, I'll get to work then," Emma said, happy that she didn't have to demolish the space gently. She had clients in the past who had wanted to sell their old kitchen, which was fine. It just meant that the demo took longer because each piece had to be delicately removed. Now she knew that she could wield her hammer any way she saw fit.

"Right, well, I'll leave you to it," Nora said, placing her hand on Emma's shoulder before she left.

The days went quickly, with Emma cleaning out the debris and keeping a tidy workspace. Nora had joined Emma in the kitchen while she worked several times, checking up on her and bringing her a soda or ice water, but Jackson preferred to stay out of the way.

"Would you like some iced tea?" Nora asked as she walked into the kitchen. Emma put her crowbar down and stepped down from her ladder.

"That would be lovely," Emma replied before she went to the bathroom to wash her hands. Looking in the mirror, she smirked at the dirty girl who stared back at her. She took the time to wash her arms and face, and dust her clothes off, not wanting to make Nora or Jackson's furniture dirty.

"Where's Jackson?" Emma asked, coming back to sit in the informal dining space where Nora had set up afternoon tea.

"Oh, he's in his study," Nora waved her hand as she spoke as if the subject was unimportant.

"He is always working and being busy. How's the kitchen coming? I hope it's not too much for you," Nora added.

"I can handle it," Emma angled her face so Nora couldn't see her turn red. "Tomorrow, going to take out the last of those cabinets. Once that's done, I can tidy everything and get started installing your new kitchen."

"Who would have thought destroying a kitchen would only take a few days," Nora giggled and poured herself a second glass. Nora glanced up at Emma, and she affectionately placed her hand on Emma's. "You must share your secret with me," Nora said, taking Emma by surprise. Emma felt the urge to pull her hand free of Nora's grip but only for a second. Nora's hand was soft, warm, and gentle. Emma realized that she didn't want to let go. She wanted to hold her hand for as long as possible.

"What secret?" She asked in a hushed tone as if she didn't want the world to know what they were talking about.

"How do you manage always to look so gorgeous?" Emma's face turned red right as the words flowed out of Nora's mouth.

"Honestly, you've been working and sweating all day, and you still look so beautiful," Nora explained. Emma burst out in a mix between loud laughter and soft giggling. She couldn't control herself. Butterflies danced around in her stomach, and a lump formed in her throat. Her face felt hot, and she was sure it was as red as a rose.

"Oh, I'm not that good," Emma managed to say between her bursts of laughter.

"I must know your secret. You look so young and beautiful all the time," Nora gushed. "Don't be so modest, Emma! You're gorgeous. You should show it to the world instead of just hiding away." Emma glanced back toward the near-empty kitchen and hoped Jackson couldn't hear them talking. She wasn't sure why it made her feel so out of place to receive a compliment from Nora. After all, they were just talking. Still, something nagged at the back of Emma's mind, telling her that this was more than just some innocent girl talk.

Emma and Nora exchanged skincare advice while finishing their tea. Nora went out shopping while Emma got back to work. She still needed to remove some of the cupboards and counters before she could call it a day.

The house seemed lifeless without Nora, and Emma felt the rest of the day go by quickly. Emma hoped Nora would come back from her shopping before she left. This seemed unlikely as Emma used her crowbar to remove the last cupboard from the wall and still heard nothing. She didn't want it to drop to the floor and disturb Jackson, who worked in his study the whole day. She tried juggling the crowbar in one hand while she held the other out to catch the cupboard before it hit the floor. She grunted under her breath and blinked away a bead of sweat dripping down her eyebrow.

"Do you need some help?" The deep, towering voice filled the silence and sent shivers up her spine. Emma gasped and looked behind her. She lost her grip on the crowbar and moved her hand away from the cupboard. The wall released the cupboard, and it fell straight to the ground, filling the room with echoes of crashing wood. Jackson stood in the doorway, staring at Emma with his dark, intense eyes. Emma looked down at the cupboard, smashed to bits on the floor, and back up at him. He stood there, still and quiet.

"I didn't mean to startle you," Jackson said, seeing the frightened look on Emma's face.

"Sorry," Emma eventually spoke, her voice shaky and soft. "I was trying to be quiet. Did I distract you from your work?" Jackson shook his head slightly.

"I'm taking a break to get a glass of water. How's everything coming along? I can see we'll be getting the new kitchen in very soon," he said.

"Yeah, it's coming along well. That was the last cupboard before I left for the day," Emma replied, wiping the sweat from her brow.

Jackson walked through the doorway and towards Emma. He stopped in front of her, towering over her small body. He was overpowering. His scent was strong and sweet, his physique helped him resemble a mountain, and his stare pierced right into Emma's soul. He leaned in close to her. Their faces were a few inches apart. Emma's body shook. She wasn't sure if it was from fear or anticipation. His warm breath tickled down her neck, and she tried hard not to breathe. His hand reached behind her and turned on the tap. He pulled a glass from behind his back and filled it with water before pulling away from her. He stood tall above her once again, but he was still close enough to smell his sweet scent.

"If you ever need any help, don't be afraid to ask," Jackson told her as he turned and walked towards the door.

"I don't want you hurting yourself or damaging those pretty hands of yours," he added. An unsure smile tugged at the corner of

Emma's lips as she whispered.

"Thank you, but I'll be fine," Emma replied.

"I hope so," Jackson smirked. "I don't think a young girl as beautiful as you should be getting dirty like this, although I do love a woman who knows how to work with her hands." Jackson left the room, and Emma was alone in silence once again. Her heart pounded in her chest, and the blood rushed to her head. Emma drew in a deep breath to calm herself, and she only noticed how cold the air around her was compared to the heat that had come off of Jackson. She shook her head clear of the thought of him as she heard the front door open and close.

"I'm home!" Nora's sweet, excited voice echoed through the grand house.
Emma sighed and relaxed. At least she would be able to say goodbye to Nora before she went home for the evening. Emma leaned down to pick up her crowbar, but she touched something

rough and sharp.

"Ouch!" She cried out as she withdrew her hand from the jagged edge of the broken cupboard. She stared at the blood dripping from her thumb in shock. Nora walked into the kitchen and dropped her bags to the floor.

"Oh, Emma, honey, you've hurt yourself!" Nora said as she rushed across the kitchen to Emma. Emma stared up at Nora as she cradled her thumb and inspected the wound.

"Don't worry, sweetie. I'll take good care of you," Nora said as she began to collect the medical supplies, she would need to clean and bandage Emma's thumb. Emma followed Nora around, numb and quiet. Nora led her upstairs to the bathroom and cleaned the blood from the cut. She cradled Emma's hand in her lap as she held a towel against it until the bleeding stopped. Emma sat and patiently waited as Nora searched through the cupboards for a plaster. She pulled out one with hearts on it and wrapped it around Emma's thumb.

"There you go, darling," Nora said as she leaned down and kissed Emma's thumb. "All better." Emma was frozen in place, and her tongue didn't want to work. She wanted to say thank you, but the words couldn't find their way out of her mouth. It felt too good. Nora took care of her, and Emma felt herself fall into little space with no effort. The effort came from trying to pull herself out of it because to be looked after the way Nora was, was all that Emma had ever wanted. Nora took one last look at Emma's hand, slowly raising her head to look at Emma deep into her eyes. The simple gesture took Emma's breath away, and she felt her world turn in slow motion, almost as if Nora had discovered her secret and that she was alright with it. The silence was broken by slow, deliberate footsteps heading for the bathroom door. Jackson appeared in the doorway and glanced between Emma and Nora.

"Hey, honey," Nora greeted him as she stood up. The energy in the room was unmissable. Jackson smirked to himself, happy that Nora had made such an impact on Emma. In their experience, it was significantly harder to find a woman who wanted both of them, more so, Nora. Usually, women threw themselves at Jackson, but it was harder to find a woman who was first, bisexual, and then secondly, who also found Nora attractive. Jackson wasn't sure what it was about her that other women seemed to find off-putting. She was gorgeous, intelligent, and caring, and still, they had yet to find a woman who both of them liked, and who liked both of them.

"Emma hurt her thumb in the kitchen," Nora's eyes told Jackson all he needed to know.

"I was worried something like that would happen," Jackson stated calmly. He looked down at Emma.

"Are you alright?" His words were more caring and sympathetic than Emma was used to hearing, and it made her tilt her head before she nodded and stared back at him. She still couldn't get her words to come out of her mouth. She watched Nora and Jackson talk about her thumb and how they don't want her to hurt herself. Emma struggled to keep her jaw from hanging open.

"I'm fine," she finally found the right words to say. She stood up and walked away from them, but feeling herself being pulled back by their loving energy.

"I'm fine. It's just a small cut. It's nothing to worry about," Emma insisted.

"Are you sure?" Jackson asked, staring down at her with his dark eyes, not believing her.

"I'm sure. Thank you for worrying about me, but you don't have to," Emma said before she picked up her jacket she had taken off while Nora was cleaning her thumb.

"I've finished for the day, so I'm going to head home. I'll see you tomorrow," Emma said, walking out of the bathroom. Nora and Jackson shared a look of concern before turning back to Emma. Nora gave her a nod of approval, and

Jackson simply stared in silence. Emma grabbed her tools, and with Jackson's help, loaded them into her truck.

Well, that was interesting, Emma thought as she began to drive home. She tried not to think about the way Nora had stroked her hand as she looked at her lovingly or the way Jackson had made sure to pick up all the heaviest tools for her. Shaking her head, she stopped to pick up something to eat on the way home.

The whole night she kept herself busy, but she couldn't get her mind off of Nora and Jackson. Emma grabbed her laptop and typed ferociously at the keys. She had a thought in her mind, and it wasn't going away until she had the proof to match it. She opened a few websites within the ABDL online community, and she put both Nora and Jackson's names into the search bar. She searched through all the websites that she knew and searched through a few that she'd only heard of. When she was about to give up, she found what she was looking for, and she sat back in her chair and almost cried tears of relief and joy. Nora and Jackson were part of the same ABDL online community that she was, *The Play Area*. Emma had probably seen their names before, and she never realized. She looked through several of their profiles and ads. They were a Mommy and Daddy, and they were looking for a little. Emma closed her laptop and looked blankly around the room. It all made sense, and yet it made no sense at all. She'd been a part of the online community for a few years now, and she had never met someone in person. Now she had met two of them and didn't even know it. She wasn't sure what to do next. Emma only knew one thing for sure; she would never look at Jackson and Nora the same way again.

Chapter 4

Emma woke up the next day, feeling exhausted. It was something else to do a kitchen demo all by herself, and her muscles were aching from deep within the tissue. She thought about asking the guys to come with her, but not enough time had passed to get over the flu. She lay in bed and thought about Nora and Jackson.

Do they know? Have they seen my profile? My ads? Oh my gosh, they must think I am so desperate! Emma thought to herself, rolling over and covering her face in her fluffy pink blankies. She ran her fingers through the soft material and sighed. Emma felt so little-triggered ever since she found out that Nora and Jackson were caregivers. It was so strange meeting someone in real life from her community. Emma checked the time, knowing that she would need to get up right away if she was to make it to the other side of town on time.

Can't be late for Mommy and Daddy,

Emma thought, rolling her eyes at herself and feeling all the feelings she knew all too well.

"Those clouds are looking kind of mean," Nora stated as she joined Emma in the kitchen. Emma jumped slightly at Nora's appearance and paused from her work to look out the window. The sky was blue the last time she checked, but it was slowly filling up with thick, dark clouds.

"It looks like we're going to have a nasty storm tonight," Emma agreed. "I might need to leave a little early so that I can get home before the rain hits. I hate driving in the rain."

"Oh, I'm the same. I always let Jackson go out for me when the weather looks like this. Why don't I ask him to drive you home? Then you don't have to worry," Nora questioned. Emma thought about it for a moment. The proposal was very alluring. She hated driving in the rain, and she was tired after a long day of cleaning out the rubble from the kitchen. It would be nice if Jackson could drive her home. Her house was almost an hour away from theirs, meaning it would be a long drive in traffic regardless. Adding the rain on top, and Emma knew that she had a 2-hour drive ahead of her.

"That's okay. If I leave early, I won't have to worry about the rain," Emma eventually said. "Thank you for the offer, though."

"Okay, as long as you're sure," Nora happily replied. She was always so kind and had a permanent smile on her face.

"Jackson should be back from the store soon. It's too bad you'll probably have to leave before he arrives. I'll say goodbye for you," Nora said before she winked at her, making Emma grin.

Oh, she knows, she knows for sure! Emma thought to herself as she waited for Nora to leave the room. She hoped she didn't insult her by turning down the offer. It was a nice gesture, but Emma didn't want to know what would happen if she was left alone with Jackson. She didn't trust herself not to mention their profile or hers for that matter. She turned away from Nora, feeling her heart pound in her chest. What she didn't see was Nora looking at her seductively as Emma bent down and started to pick up her tools.

The sky was completely dark, and it was drizzling by the time Emma started packing her tools in the truck. She moved fast so she could get home before the real rain began to pour. She was happy that she was such a tidy worker as the kitchen debris had all been cleared away, and all that was left was a spotless working space for the beginning of installation in the morning.

"I'll be fine," Emma assured Nora as Nora leaned against the truck. However, her uncertainty was evident in her voice. Nora just raised an eyebrow, and Emma smirked at how sassy Nora could become.

"Don't worry about me. I'll see you tomorrow morning," Emma insisted. Emma had to admit; she liked the worried attention she received from Nora. It felt nice to have someone worry and care about her.

"Please drive safely," Nora said, finally standing back from the truck and folding her arms over her chest as Emma slowly drove away. She drove down the cobblestone driveway and onto the highway. She was still an hour away but hoped the highway would help her get there before the weather got worse.

As Emma drove, she turned on her headlights. The clouds made it dark, and the cold fogged her windshield. She used the air-conditioning to clear the mist and turned the radio off to keep her focus. The rain started to come down harder. She gripped the steering wheel tight, making her knuckles turn white, and her arms shook violently. She wasn't a confident driver at all, especially not in this big truck. She moved to the slow lane and took her foot off the gas. People honked as they passed her. The wind picked up, and the rain turned into hard hail. The rain and hail slammed against the car. She couldn't see a thing, not even with her lights on. Deciding that it might be best to wait the storm out, she pulled off the highway and stopped on the side of the road at the first chance she got and turned the engine off. The rain poured down hard, so she kept her hazard lights on. She had managed to park under a clump of trees hoping that the truck wouldn't suffer too much damage.

"Damn it," she muttered as she pulled out her phone. "No reception? You've got to be kidding me!" Emma sat back in the car and turned the engine back on. She used it to keep the heat on, and for the headlights, the last thing she needed was somebody ramming the truck from behind because they couldn't see her. She wasn't sure where she had turned off the highway, but it seemed like a dirt road to nowhere. She hoped someone would drive past soon and stop to help her.

But I mean, what are they even going to do it they stop? It's not like they can control the storm, Emma said to herself. She closed her eyes and replayed the images of Nora and Jackson to try and calm herself down. She sunk into the seat and began thinking of them rescuing her.

"Come to Daddy," she imagined Jackson saying if she was to turn around and knock on their front door.

"Oh, what a wet little girl. Let's get you all warmed up, baby," she thought of Nora saying, taking her hand and leading her into the bathroom. She imagined Jackson running her a warm bubble bath. Nora would begin to undress her, running her fingertips over her wet, soft skin giving her goosebumps and letting her snuggle into her neck.

"Mommy's got you," Nora would say, just before Jackson would pick her up in his strong, muscular arms and put her into the bath. Playing with the bubbles, Emma imaged that she would race her bath toys around the tub, happily dancing as Jackson played a chilled playlist throughout the house. Nora sat by the tub, and lazily ran her hand through the water as she kept

Emma company.

"Isn't this better than being all by yourself, little girl. You just need Mommy and Daddy, and we aren't going to let you out of our sights," Nora would say as Jackson took a warm towel and lifted Emma out of the tub and dried her as he carried her through the house and into their bedroom.

Emma hadn't noticed the car which had slowed down and stopped behind her. A knock came on her window, and she startled as she saw a tall figure standing outside her window. She was about to drive away out of fear, only stopping once she saw the figure bend down and Jackson's intense stare looking straight at her. She pressed her window down. Emma smile at Jackson, who had wrapped his trench coat around himself. The rainwater dripping off his peaked cap made him look even cooler than he usually did.

"Interesting way of spending your afternoon," Jackson joked, making Emma laugh.

Emma wasn't sure what to say or do. It was the first time she had ever seen him smile properly, and it was the first time he said something resembling a joke. A smile of her own pulled at the corner of her lips.

"Wow! What a coincidence," she laughed.

"You want a lift back to our place? I just heard the forecast, and the rain looks like it'll be here for a few hours yet," Jackson said, causing Emma to bite her bottom lip and slowly nod her head.

He knows, Emma thought as she unlocked the truck and began to load the tools into the back of Jackson's car.

"This is kind of you, thanks. Are you sure that Nora won't mind?" Emma asked, worried that she would be an inconvenience to them. Jackson put the heater up for Emma and gave her his waistcoat to keep warm. Her work clothes were soaked, but she had her everyday clothes in her bag. She always kept a bag of clothes with her, throwback behavior to her troubled childhood.

"No. in fact, I think that she'll be delighted. I don't even want to think of the hell she would have given me if I had told her that I drove past you sitting on the side of the road by yourself," Jackson replied, placing his hand on Emma's thigh and squeezing it gently before going back to driving with two hands.

"Sorry, I," Jackson said, not wanting Emma to think that he had only offered her safety in exchange for sex.

"No, it's okay. I don't want to home wreck or anything, but you guys are so beautiful and handsome and gorgeous," Emma blurted out, making Jackson laugh and nod his head. Emma sat in silence and closed her eyes for the rest of the drive back to their home. She was relieved to have been saved and happy to be heading back to Nora and Jackson's house. It felt as though a weight had been lifted from her shoulders, but she checked herself, not wanting to be reading too much into the situation.

***

"You're soaked to the bone! You poor thing!" Nora cried out as Jackson hurried Emma inside the house. "You should have stayed here, to begin with. This is horrible weather. I should have tried to be more convincing that you should have stayed!" Nora exclaimed. Emma loved that they both seemed to care about her, but she tried to brush it off as nothing more than standard care and concern any kind human would have for another.

They are just nice. You are reading way too much into this. They probably do this with everyone who works for them. This is not your fantasy, Emma tried to remind herself, but she had to admit, it was quite close to the fantasy she had had only 30minutes ago. Emma wasn't sure what to say, so she just let out a soft, lighthearted giggle.

"Jackson will make you a nice, warm cup

of tea while I run you a hot bath. How does that sound?" Nora walked Emma up the stairs while Jackson disappeared into the makeshift kitchen area.

"That sounds nice," Emma responded softly. "But you don't have to do that. I can just have a quick shower and change."

"Don't be silly! I want you to have a proper soak in the bath to get that frost from your bones. Otherwise, you might get sick," Nora insisted, refusing to take no for an answer this time. Something told Emma that she was better off listening to Nora and Jackson. Emma decided not to protest further as Nora led her through the house. This was the first time she saw the house in its entirety. The upstairs was just as large and luxurious as the downstairs, and Emma had a hard time acting like their home was nothing out of the ordinary.

She sat in her wet clothes while Nora ran her a hot bath and waited for her to leave the room before she undressed and got in. The water warmed her from the inside out. She sunk into it until only her nose was above the water. She breathed the steam in, and she could feel it healing her with every breath.

"Hey there, sweetie," Nora's voice came from the other side of the bathroom door and a soft knock.

"Can I come in? I have your tea," she asked. Emma sat up slightly and moved the bubbles close to her so they could hide her body.

"Yeah, you can come in," Emma replied. Nora opened the door slowly and walked in. She placed a modern-looking silver tray down on the small wooden table and moved it close so Emma could reach it. She poured the tea into the small, china cup and handed it to Emma.

"Are you feeling better?" Nora asked her. Emma remained hidden by the bubbles as she lifted her hand to take the teacup. She nodded her head while she beamed a smile at Nora.

"I'm feeling a lot better, thank you for all of this," Emma quietly replied. She could feel her mind betray her and lead her into little space, the one headspace she didn't want to be in at that moment.

"Jackson was anxious about you," Nora continued as she sat on the edge of the bath, excited at the thought of seeing Emma naked.

"He was glad that he found you. You know you're welcome to stay here whenever you want. We'd rather make up the spare room for you than risk you driving home in the rain," Nora explained.

"Thank you very much," Emma shuffled in the bath and glanced down to make sure the bubbles were still in place. "I'll keep that in mind next time."

"I'll get your clothes from your bag and leave them by the door. Don't be afraid to call out if you need anything," Nora gently said, smiling down at Emma. Nora left Emma alone in the bath once again. Emma relaxed a bit more and held her cup of tea close to her chest. She breathed in the sweet scent before taking a sip. It warmed her from the inside, and the bath warmed her outside. Her aching muscles felt as ease, and all memory of being lost out in the storm disappeared from her mind and body. The night went on slowly, and the bathwater grew cold. Emma decided that it was time for her to rejoin the world and leave her small spot of comfort. She found her bag right outside the bathroom door and grabbed it quickly. She was dry and dressed in a few minutes before she headed downstairs to look for Jackson and Nora. She found them in the living room.

"There you are," Nora said when she spotted Emma in the doorway. "We've been waiting for you. I got dinner ready. I'll throw it into the oven to warm up, and we can all sit down to eat."

"You don't have to do that," Emma tried to hurry after Nora as she rushed towards the kitchen.

"Nonsense!" Jackson interrupted. "We insist. Now come and sit down while Nora gets dinner ready." Jackson put his hands on Emma's shoulders and led her to the dining table. He pulled a chair out and sat her down before returning to his seat. Emma felt strange. She was uncomfortable and relaxed at the same time. It was nice that they were taking care of her and didn't need to do anything, but she didn't want to take too much from them.

"I don't want to be an inconvenience or anything," Emma stated so that Jackson knew how she felt.

"You're not an inconvenience, you're our guest," Jackson assured her. "We're happy to make you feel comfortable, so just relax and let us take care of you." Jackson was so powerful and strong when he spoke. He made Emma feel like he had the last say, and there was no point in arguing with him. She decided to do just that. She leaned back in her chair and relaxed until Nora came back into the room. She carried in trays of meat and vegetables before going back out and bringing back more trays with gravy and potatoes.

"This looks amazing. How did you cook it all?!" Emma questioned.

"I didn't cook it silly. We don't have a kitchen," Nora giggled as she placed a plate in front of Emma. "This is just some of the stuff I asked Jackson to get from the store. All I did was throw it in the oven," Nora and Jackson dished some of the food on to their plates, but Emma felt awkward leaning over the table to fill her own. Jackson looked over and saw that she wasn't getting any food for herself. She watched him get up from his seat, walk around to her side of the table, and grab her plate.

"You should eat plenty of vegetables and meat. You need it after the big week you've had," Jackson told her as he dished her up some food.

"If you eat all of your dinner, there's some ice-cream and cake for dessert," Nora said, surprising Emma. Jackson sat back down, and Emma watched them both begin to eat. She thought about how she found their names on the

ABDL online community and how they acted a lot like how she would expect a Mommy and Daddy to behave. She ate her food slowly. She wanted to mention it somehow, without seeming weird. After all, there could be plenty of Nora's and Jacksons out there, and it might not be them that she found online. But she needed to know. She couldn't go on eating across the table from them without knowing for certain who they were.

"You two are very hospitable," Emma started to say, pausing for a second. She knew where the conversation needed to go, but couldn't find the words at first.

"You're kind of like a Mommy and Daddy," she knew that it was a risk, but the words escaped her lips before she had a chance to stop them. Emma threw in a laugh at the end to make it seem like a joke. Nora and Jackson both paused in the middle of placing spoonful's of food into their mouths. They put their utensils down and shared a look that Emma couldn't make out. She wasn't sure if they were angry, concerned, or just confused. She watched them intently, awaiting their answer. Nora gave Jackson a slight nod of approval, and Jackson turned to face Emma once more. His eyes stared deeply into hers, and she was captured by them.

"Here's the thing, Emma," Jackson began, his voice carrying a hint of tenderness but still filled with intense power. "We are, a Mommy and Daddy, as you put it."

"And we know that you're a little," Nora added. "We saw your name online, but we weren't going to say anything because we know how sensitive people can be about coming out in public."

"What do you mean?" Emma asked, trying to act as if this conversation wasn't making her cheeks go hot, and she hoped they weren't as red as they felt.

"How long have you known I'm a little?" Emma said, seeing the look on Nora and Jackson's face, realizing that her attempts were futile.

"We only found out after we hired you to reinstall the kitchen," Jackson explained calmly. "We didn't hire you because we knew you were a little."

"We were keeping quiet because we've had problems with little's in the past, not wanting anything more than an online relationship," Nora explained. "We understand that, of course. So we kept our knowledge of you a secret."

"I'm not one of those people," Emma defended herself as if they had insulted her.

"I have problems with Mommies and Daddies not wanting anything more than an online relationship. I am not like that." Nora and Jackson looked at each other once again, and Emma began to feel as though they could share thoughts. She waited patiently for one of them to say something, but her patience was fading. Nora finally got up from her chair and moved it next to Emma. She sat down and leaned in close to Emma. Jackson stayed where he was and watched the two of them closely.

"You know, Emma, Jackson, and I have been looking for a little to play with for some time now," Nora whispered to her. "As we said before, no one wants to take the relationship further than online, and very few of them are comfortable with having both a Mommy and a Daddy."

"Well…" Emma glanced up at Jackson before returning her gaze at Nora. "I wouldn't mind that. I think it would be great to have both a Mommy and a Daddy to play with." Nora's face lit up as she sat up in her chair. She looked over at Jackson, who even allowed a smile to spread across his face.

"Emma, do you want to play with us tonight and see how we all like it?" Jackson asked her. His voice was soft as silk, and it spoke to her soul. Nora's face was soft and gleeful. Emma couldn't help the wide grin spreading across her face. She was done with the online fakes telling her that they wanted something and then backing out at the last second. She only ever wanted something real. Now they were sitting right in front of her, and they wanted something real too.

The three discussed their likes and dislikes as the continued dinner, agreeing on a safe word and talking briefly about their limits. They all decided that moving slowly was the best idea for them and slowly began to slip into more, deliberate dynamic play.

"Do you want some dessert, baby girl?" Nora asked her. "Have you eaten all of your vegetables?" Emma lifted her plate proudly to show that all of her vegetables have been eaten. Nora took the plate, pretended to inspect it, and then patted Emma on the head.

"That's a perfect, little one!" She cheered before walking into the kitchen.

Emma wrapped her hands around the edge of her seat and kicked her legs back and forth playfully. She couldn't remember the last time she felt this relaxed and happy. The weight of the world and all the responsibilities that came with it melted away, and she could just be the little girl she felt like inside.

"What do you want to do after dessert?" Jackson asked her. "We can watch a movie or play some games."

"I like to play games!" Emma jumped in her seat. "What games do you have?"

"I like Monopoly," Nora's voice traveled through the house from the kitchen. Jackson leaned over the table and whispered in Emma's ear, "Don't worry, she's not very good at Monopoly. She always wants to borrow money from the bank."

"I just have one question," Emma said seriously, breaking out into giggles as she added, "Can I please be the puppy?" Jackson smiled, the warmth in his eyes melting Emma and giving her a shiver down her spine.

They finished their dessert, and Emma waited while Jackson set up the Monopoly board. They played a long game of Monopoly that lasted well into the night. Jackson was a strict banker, but he kept sneaking Emma money underneath the table, helping Emma win the game.

"Baby, you won!" Nora exclaimed, pulling Emma into her lap and kissing her cheek. Emma giggled, Jackson, deciding that he didn't want the evening to end. He packed the board away and turned on a movie.

"If it gets too scary, you can snuggle into us," he said, draping a blanket over Emma. While it was not the most play filled evening, the shift in power dynamic was enough to send them all into their respective headspaces. Nora and Jackson cuddled on the couch while Emma rested her head on their laps. They watched the film while the hailstorm raged outside. Emma felt safe and warm in their arms and was surprised at how easily she entered her little space. She didn't want to rush into anything too quickly, but as she closed her eyes and fell asleep, she couldn't wait to see where this new dynamic would take her.

Chapter 5

"Emma!" Nora cried out Monday morning, running down the front stairs. Emma got out of the truck just as Nora jumped at her and threw her arms around her neck. Jackson marched down the stairs slowly to join them in the driveway. Emma glanced at the truck to her side. The delivery men had already begun unloading the counters, and she winced to see them being placed directly on the ground. She made a mental note to deal with that later.

"The counters are beautiful!" Nora cheered, finally releasing Emma from her warm embrace. "And the cupboards are just wonderful. I can't wait to see what they look like when they're put together."

"Neither can I," Emma agreed. "I better get started!"

"It's nice to see you again," Jackson spoke softly as he reached the bottom of the staircase. "Nora and I have been discussing doing something with you the whole week. Haven't we?"

"Oh, yes," Nora excitedly said and grabbed hold of Emma's hand. "Jackson and I would like to take you out somewhere."

"Really?" Emma's face lit up, and she felt like a kid on Christmas morning. "Where are you going to take me?"

"It's a surprise," Jackson whispered. Emma was ready to throw everything away and jump into their car, but there was still a full day of work to complete.

The day went by quickly, and soon the delivery truck was gone. Emma looked at her handiwork, displayed by marble counters and backlit cupboards. She was proud of herself for managing to do this job alone. It was always her and the guys. She never worked by herself, but she always knew that she could handle it. It still didn't make the job any easier. Her body was tired, and she felt as though all she did was work, eat and sleep. So when Nora had suggested that Emma have a shower after her workday because they were going to take her on an adventure, she jumped at the chance.

Jackson held the back door open for Emma before getting into the driver's seat. It was a strange feeling, not knowing where she was going, but Emma was excited about the surprise. She thought of all the things it could be. The first thing that came to mind was a trip to the park, but Emma saw how the car had been packed and knew that wasn't right. They were taking her somewhere really special, and the thought made all the hair on Emma's neck stand up.
She was practically bouncing in her seat as Jackson drove. They were near the beach now, and Emma could see the seagulls flying over the car. She leaned her head out the window and watched them glide against the wind. The sounds of the waves crashing against the shore grew closer. Jackson turned the corner, and right in

front of them, Emma spotted the very top of a
Ferris wheel over the hill in the distance.

"A theme park!" Emma cheered as she
realized where they were going. "You're taking
me to a theme park?" Nora nodded, "I knew you
would be excited." They drove directly to the
park, and Emma couldn't stop jumping up and
down in her seat. This was the best thing anyone
had ever done for her. Her parents wouldn't even
take her to a theme park when she was a child.
She couldn't wait to open up the door and run
into the park, but the child lock was on, so she
had to wait for Jackson to open the door for her.

"Now, here are the rules," Jackson
explained as Emma climbed out of the car. "You
stay within our sight at all times, don't wander
off. You ask nicely before you go on any rides or
play any games. If you're a good girl, Nora and I
will buy you all the toys and treats you want.
Okay?" Emma was excited that they wanted to
continue their dynamic and looked up at Jackson
as she realized what kind of outing this was. She

beamed up at him and nodded her head in response. She could already tell this was going to be the best day.

Emma was deep in her little space as she ran from one ride to the next. She kept her eyes on Nora and Jackson, so she didn't stray too far from them or break any rules. They went on the rollercoaster first. Emma squeezed into the seats between Nora and Jackson, and they each held her hand during the scary parts. Jackson played a strongman game and won her a giant panda toy. Nora went with her on the teacup ride because Jackson was too tall for it. Emma just wanted to spend the whole day there and never leave.

After trying many of the rides, Nora and Jackson suggested they get something for dinner.

"You've been a really good girl today, Emma, so you get to choose what we have for dinner," Nora told her and pinched her cheek playfully.

"Can we have pizza and chocolate

milkshakes, please?" Emma gasped. "And can we eat it on the Ferris wheel?" It was always a dream of Emma's, although she never told anyone about it.

"I think that's a great idea," Jackson agreed. He looked down at her as she hugged her giant panda toy, and she couldn't be happier. Emma sat on the opposite end of the car as it slowly rose into the air. She wanted to stand up and look over the edge, but Jackson and Nora told her to sit down and stay locked into her seatbelt.

"This has been the best day ever," Emma told them as they opened the pizza box. "I don't want this day to end."

"The day doesn't have to end, but we do need to leave the park before it closes," Nora giggled. "It was such a long drive coming here. Maybe we should stay the night." Emma's face lit up, and Jackson let out a chuckle, "I think that's our answer to that."

"Then it's settled! We'll get a room and

stay the night," Nora replied.

"But actually, what about the kitchen? I have to work on it tomorrow," Emma asked, realizing that she had grown up jobs that needed to be completed.

"You are such a good girl, but I think we can wait one extra day to have the kitchen ready," Jackson said, sweeping the hair out of her eyes and putting her mind at ease.

"Now, don't eat too much pizza, or you'll feel sick," he added, leaning forward and taking a huge, Daddy size bite from her slice, making her giggle.

The weather grew colder, and Jackson had to lend Emma his jacket. Nora and Jackson kept their word because Emma had followed all of the rules for the afternoon. They stayed at the theme park until they were told to leave before closing time. They let Emma play almost all the games, and she won lots of prizes. They rode all the rides at least twice, and Emma was full from cotton candy, popcorn, and soda. When they left, Jackson dropped Nora and Emma off at the closest restaurant to make a reservation while he searched the small town for a decent hotel.

"Now, you wait here while I go in and make a reservation for later," Nora instructed Emma once Jackson had driven off.

"If you're good and you don't wander off, then Mommy will take let you do some shopping before Daddy comes back," Nora instructed. This was the first time that she had referred to herself as Mommy or Jackson Daddy, and it filled Emma with a warmth she was not expecting to feel.

"I'll be good for you, Mommy," Emma said with a large, proud grin. Nora winked at her before she patted her on the head and walked into the restaurant. Emma let out a sigh when she was far away. She'd been holding in that breath all day long. It was a good sigh, a happy sigh. Emma was the happiest she had ever been in a long time, and she couldn't imagine herself getting happier.

When Nora returned and saw Emma in the same spot, they walked across the street and searched the nearby shops. They were quick, so they would be back in time for Jackson to pick them up. Nora took Emma to two different clothing shops and brought her several new outfits, complete with hats and jewelry. Nora had such good taste, and she picked all of the clothes for Emma.

When they were done, they loaded the bags into the car, and Jackson drove them to the hotel he found. They checked into their room, and Emma tried on all of the outfits that Nora bought her to show Jackson.

"This one's my favorite!" Emma told them as she danced out of the bathroom wearing a pink dress with a low cut back that had Jackson's full attention, making Nora smirk.

"That one's my favorite, too," Nora agreed. "What do you think, Jackson?"

"I like it," Jackson stated in his subtle,

calm voice, but his eyes and growing bulge suggested that he would rather it be on the floor instead of on Emma.

"I think you should wear it to dinner tonight," he said as he stood up from the edge of the bed and grabbed his keys.

"We should get going before we miss our reservation," he added, the bulge unmissable, turning Emma on when she realized he had no intention of trying to hide it.

***

The sun rose by the ocean side and reflected off the blue, calm waves. Emma was awake early, and she sat on the balcony and watched the colors light up the sky one by one as the day began. The street below was quiet but busy. Almost no one in the small beachside town owned a car, so they walked everywhere. They kept the roads clear and the morning calm. She thought about the day she had before, the trip to the theme park, the shopping spree with Nora, and the dinner last night. It was perfect. She didn't want it to end, but she knew that at some point, it must.

"Emma, you're awake already?" Nora walked out onto the balcony and joined her. "I thought you would want to sleep in. We don't have any plans today, remember so you can relax all day."

"I like watching the sun," Emma told her. "I know we did a lot yesterday, but I don't feel tired at all." Although they did do a lot the previous day, they hadn't done the one thing that Emma's body was craving. Especially when Jackson had pulled her up onto his lap and spread her thighs, pushing his bulge along her panty covered pussy as they ate ice cream by the ocean. Emma remembered how he had bounced her on his lap, reaching under her dress and spreading her cheeks as he grinded against her, making her feel more of him whispering, *Mommy likes watching you be Daddy's good little girl.*

"I'm glad you aren't tired," Nora let out a soft giggle. "Let's wait for Jackson to wake up, and we'll see what we're going to do today." Emma nodded and returned to watching the sunrise.

When Jackson woke up, she and Nora joined him in the bedroom. Nora crawled in next to him, and Emma sat on the edge of the bed. She crossed her legs and waited for what Nora and Jackson decided.

"What would you like to do today?" Nora asked him, amused that her mind had already put both Jackson and Emma into several sexual positions, wondering if that was something that could happen this morning. He thought for a moment.

"I have a few ideas," he replied, understanding his wife's tone of voice.

"We can go to the theme park again," Emma suggested hopefully. "I'll be good, I promise."

"We can go to the theme park again if you want to, but maybe later today, after breakfast," Jackson spoke calmly. Emma didn't want to show them she was disappointed, so she nodded in agreement. Nora noticed and crawled across the bed to meet her at the edge.

"We can still have fun until then," she whispered in Emma's ear. Emma wasn't sure what was happening at first, but it became very clear when Nora started kissing down the side of her neck. Her eyes glanced up at Jackson, and he sat back and watched Nora with intense eyes.

"Is this okay?" Nora whispered as her lips moved down to Emma's collar bone, and her hands pulled the top of her shirt aside. Emma swallowed the lump forming in her throat and tried to calm the heart beating hard against her chest. There was no way she could control her breathing. It was hard and shaky as Nora's soft, warm lips gently touched her skin.

"Yeah, this is okay," she managed to reply

in a broken voice. This is what she had wanted, but there was something surreal about it finally happening. Nora's hand slipped down Emma's shirt and gently cupped her breast. Nora squeezed, and Emma moaned instinctively. Nora's hands were gentle and soft; they warmed her from the inside out.

Emma watched Jackson's hand move beneath the covers and move up and down by his shaft. He quickly grew hard under the duvet as he watched Nora play with Emma's breasts. Emma watched him play with himself, and it made her wet and feel tingly inside.

He grew tired of watching and threw the covers aside. He was completely naked, and Emma got a full view of his enlarged penis, pointing aggressively at her and coming towards her, to claim her. Jackson pushed his lips against Emma's, and she nearly fell back from the force. He pushed himself on top of her and moved his hand down into her shorts. Jackson pulled her underwear to the side and pressed his fingers against her clit. She gasped as he moved his fingers around in circles.

"Do you want to take, Daddy?" Jackson asked, smiling at her lovingly, so she didn't feel like she needed to say yes. Nora helped her slide her legs out and laid her down on the bed as she nodded her head.

"Yes, Daddy," Emma said, the cheeky smile escaping her lips. She had been worried about Nora and Jackson becoming jealous of each other and had held back her naturally flirtatious ways, as not to rock the boat. Yet seeing both of them want her, she knew that she didn't need to hold back anymore. Jackson climbed on top of her, keeping his fingers pressed against her, and his lips stuck on hers. Nora leaned in and reached for Jackson's cock. She rubbed it up and down from the base to the tip. Jackson groaned softly and put more pressure on Emma's clit.

Emma felt as though she was doing nothing, but that's what they wanted. They wanted to please her, to take her, to use her body. They wanted her to lie there while they worked to satisfy themselves. Emma moaned and gripped the duvet as Jackson pressed against her.

"I want you," Jackson demanded as he removed his hand and pulled her shorts down. He parted her pussy lips and pushed himself inside of her and stretched her out wide. She gasped when she felt him enter. He was long and thick, and her pussy was small, but it felt good to feel filled. He pushed in deep, but he was slow and gentle. She cried out as he rocked back and forth, pressing his cock deep inside her and pulling it out.

Nora pushed in and pressed her lips against Emma's. She parted Emma's lips with her tongue and pushed her tongue into her mouth. Emma pushed her tongue back, and their tongues danced around each other in her mouth. The feeling continued to build up inside of her, and it wanted to burst. She arched her back and cried out, releasing Nora's lips.

Jackson grabbed Nora and moved her in front of him. She bent down on her knees over Emma, and he pushed his cock inside of her from behind. He moved back and forth, pushing his cock hard and fast into her. Nora leaned down and rested her mouth over Emma's pussy. Emma gasped once again at the new feeling of Nora's tongue pressed against her clit. Nora swirled her tongue around and moved it up and down. The passion grew stronger, and Emma couldn't stop herself from crying out, "Yes! Yes! Oh my God, yes!"

Jackson growled and groaned louder as he slapped his body against Nora's. He was getting close, and he knew that both Nora and Emma were too. Emma's back arched once again as the feeling inside of her became too large to hold. It exploded inside her as she threw her head back and screamed. Jackson threw his head back and cried out as he pulled out of Nora and pushed into Emma, squirting his hot cum inside Emma. Emma dug her nails into the bed as she felt the warm liquid shoot into her.

Jackson slowed his thrusts until he came to a complete stop. Emma's clit was so sensitive that each touch made her jolt. Nora pulled away from her and collapsed on the bed beside her. Jackson breathed heavily, but he too relaxed on the other side of Emma. He moved in close to her, and they cuddled her from both sides.

Emma allowed the feeling to make her weak and limp. She curled into Nora's chest, and Jackson wrapped his arms around them both from behind. They lay there together until it was time to go down for breakfast.

Chapter 6

Emma let out a soft, long sigh as she lifted the box of tiles off the truck and brought them into the kitchen, placing them on the floor. No matter how hard Emma worked, she felt she was never going to finish the kitchen. It was a four-person job, and doing it all by herself meant that she took four times as long. Deciding that it was alright that it took so long, she stopped being so hard on herself. She let out another sigh as she grabbed the broom. That was the tenth sigh this morning. She realized she'd been sighing all day, every day since Wednesday morning. She had arrived at Jackson and Nora's house early to accept and sign for the tile delivery, but something seemed wrong. There wasn't anything different about Nora or Jackson, but Emma felt like things were coming to an end. Their date had lasted days, but it was over now, making Emma wonder if their relationship would also be over soon. She sighed one more time, hoping someone would hear and ask what's wrong, but she wasn't even sure what she would say if they asked.

She swept until the kitchen floor was clean, and she scraped what was left of the old kitchen off the walls. Then she filled a bucket with warm water and cleaned the walls. Once it was dry, the new kitchen was ready to install.

"Knock, knock," Nora's voice cheered as she fake knocked on the empty doorway. "How's it going in here?" Emma sat back on her haunches and plastered a grin on her face. It felt fake and probably looked that way, "Everything's going great! I'm just about to make a start on putting the new kitchen in."

"Such a quiet job," Nora leaned against the doorway, but she didn't want to walk into the kitchen and get in Emma's way.

"I was expecting to hear banging and cutting and all sorts of sounds, but not a peep. We couldn't even tell you were here," Nora added. Emma's fake grin faded a bit, but she forced it to stay, "Oh, that's the point. I don't want to bother you guys too much."

"Don't worry about us, baby, just get your work done. That's the most important thing right now," Nora walked out before stopping suddenly and pulled back. "I'm going to go to the store quickly. Should I get you something to eat?"

"I brought my lunch today, so you don't have to worry," Emma barely looked back at Nora while she spoke. She was so busy that she didn't see Nora frown as she left the room. Emma finished installing the cupboards faster than she thought she would, making her smile as she looked at her handy work. As she screwed on the last cupboard handle, she let out yet another sigh. It was becoming a habit for her. She allowed herself a break, sitting down, and beginning to eat her lunch. Nora came back from the store and joined Emma for lunch.

"What did you pack yourself?" Nora asked her. Emma quickly swallowed her mouthful before answering, "Just some rice and chicken."

"I got some pizza if you want to share," Nora suggested, showing her the box. "You know I won't be able to eat the whole thing by myself. I also got some donuts for dessert." Emma had to think for a moment. It was all very enticing, but Emma didn't want to get too used to something she didn't think would last. She didn't allow herself to think about too much.

"No, that's okay. I'll just eat what I brought," Emma replied. "Thank you for the offer, though." Nora's brow furrowed for a second, but she quickly dismissed the feeling and returned to her usual, bubbly self.

"If that's what you want. Just make sure you are getting enough protein. You're doing a lot of work, and I don't want you getting lightheaded because you haven't eaten well enough," Nora instructed. Nora waited by Emma's side for a while, but she didn't reply. Emma kept eating her packed lunch while looking into the kitchen. Nora couldn't help but notice the grim look in her eye. Something was bothering Emma, and Nora needed to find out what it was.

Nora put her shopping away and headed up to Jackson's study. Jackson was always better at dealing with people than Nora. That's what made him a good partner. She has a creative influence, and he dealt with the people, so she didn't have to. Jackson always loved that she was so soft and caring, but that also meant that she could be a pushover.

She knocked on his study door and waited.

"Come!" Jackson's voice traveled through the door.

Nora opened the door, slipped inside, and closed it behind her quickly. She locked it, even though she knew Emma wouldn't be coming up to bother them.

"We have a problem," Nora started.

"A problem?" Jackson put his pen down and paid full attention to Nora. "A problem with what? Is it the kitchen?"

"No, it's got nothing to do with the kitchen. There's something wrong with Emma," Nora began to explain as she walked to Jackson's desk and sat down.

"She's acting differently. She's acting almost distant as if she doesn't want to be here. She's acting like she doesn't want me around," Nora said, full of self-pity.

"Have you been crowding her?" Jackson sighed and rubbed his eyes with his fingers. "You know we've talked about this. People need their space. Not everyone is like you. They don't like to be crowded."

"No, I have not crowded her. I simply asked if she wanted to have lunch with me. I even brought her favorite pizza and donuts, but she turned me down to eat her packed lunch. That's just what happened today. She's been acting strange since we were coming back from the theme park. Haven't you noticed how often she sighs? She sighs all of the time, and she probably doesn't even know that I can hear her.

Something is wrong with her, Jackson! I think she doesn't want us to take care of her anymore," Nora explained.

"That is a bit strange," Jackson mumbled. He leaned back in his chair and thought for a moment. "I'll check it out. Leave her alone for the rest of the day and let her finish her work in the kitchen. I'll check up on her when she's done and see if she is acting strange or not."
Nora squealed and jumped up. She ran around the desk and wrapped her arms around Jackson's neck. She squeezed him tight before letting go.

"Thank you, Jackson! I just hope she's okay," Nora had a skip in her step as she made her way back to the door. "I'll let you get back to work, sweetie," she blew a kiss his way before unlocking the door and stepping out.
Jackson sat by himself and thought of Emma for a moment before returning to his work. If she is acting distant, then he wanted to get to the bottom of it. Having Emma in his and Nora's life

has changed them for the better. He didn't want to lose her.

He stayed in his office until the end of the workday. He carefully watched his clock, waiting for the time when Emma usually started to pack her tools in her truck and get ready to leave. She would normally come to his study to let him know that she is finished. Today, he met her at the bottom of the stairs.

"Hello, Emma, done already," Jackson greeted her as she left the kitchen.

"Oh! Hi, Jackson, yes I'm finished for the day. Tomorrow I'll put the counters on and install the appliances," Emma replied. Emma was not only a carpenter but also an electrician. Having multiple trades was a necessity to work in this particular company.

"Would...would you like to stay for dinner? You can sleep over if you want. We can play some games, and I saw that Nora purchased a new coloring book for you. She knows how much you love those," Jackson asked, his smiling full of love. This was the first time that Emma had seen a vulnerability from Jackson, and it made her feel terrible that she had made him unsure of her affection toward him.

Emma hesitated, and Jackson noticed. Emma looked up at him as he towered over her. She felt overwhelmed by his powerful stance and position. Jackson always knew where to stand in a room to hold power over everyone else nearby. That was one of the things Emma liked about him, but it was also something that scared her.

"I don't know if it's a good idea," Emma spoke unsurely. "I don't want us to get used to things the way they are."

"Why would that be a problem?" Jackson asked.

Emma hesitated again and avoided looking directly at Jackson when she finally spoke.

"Things don't always stay the same. Some things come to an end, and I don't want to get used to it if I know that one day it's going to end," Emma replied, making Jackson's heart hurt.

"Why would you think that this will come to an end?" Jackson walked further down the stairs until he was on the same level as Emma. She finally looked directly at him.

"Have Nora and I given you a reason to think that this might end?" He asked the concern in his voice, making Emma feel like a horrible person for pushing them away.

"No, not exactly...I just know from experience that good things never last," Emma sighed and looked away again.

"Let us take you out for dinner," Jackson suggested. Emma opened her mouth to reply, and he somehow knew that she was about to decline the offer, so he interrupted her.

"I understand if you're too tired to go tonight. Let us take you out for dinner tomorrow night. Nora and I will pick you up, and we'll treat you to any restaurant you want. Is that okay?" Jackson asked, his grin reassuring.

Emma paused for a moment and thought about

it. She didn't want to say no to Jackson, so she nodded her head and gave him the slightest smile, "Okay, tomorrow night works for me." Jackson sighed out of relief. He escorted Emma to her truck and waved goodbye before returning to the house, where Nora was impatiently waiting.

"You're right," Jackson told her, "Something is wrong. We'll see if we can find out what it is tomorrow when we take her out to dinner."

***

True to his word, he and Nora picked Emma up from her apartment the next night and drove to the restaurant she chose. Emma wasn't sure what the night would entail. She didn't know if this was a date or just a dinner. She wasn't sure if she was allowed to be a little, and they were her Mommy and Daddy or if she was just Emma, and they were Nora and Jackson. She didn't know what to think anymore.

She knew they were worried about her. She wondered if they noticed how often she'd been sighing over the past few days. She suspected that she would find out at dinner.

They arrived at her favorite Chinese restaurant that the guys took her to every year for her birthday. She thought about it for a while before she finally decided on this restaurant. It held such good memories in her past that she didn't want what might happen tonight to ruin the overall atmosphere. If it were terrible, maybe the feel of the restaurant would soften the blow. They were greeted at the door and guided to their chosen table at the back of the building, near the balcony. This gave Emma a perfect view of the city's nightlife. She loved people watching. The city can be so strange and wonderful, and even more so at night.

When the waiter left, Nora grabbed the menu and handed it to Emma.

"There you go! You can have whatever you want," Nora told her.

"Anything I want?" Emma doubled checked with her, peering over the top of the menu.

"Anything! You've been a very good girl, so we're going to treat you properly tonight," Jackson said.

"Alright," Emma sighed and put the menu down. "I think I'll get my usual. It is my favorite."

"What's wrong, Emma," Jackson got straight to it, as he wasn't the type to dance around the issue. "You've been acting strange lately. Nora and I have noticed a lot of sighing and distant behavior. That's why we asked you out to this dinner, so we can discuss what's been going on," Jackson said. Although he wasn't afraid to address the tough issues, he did it in such a loving way; Emma knew deep in her heart that she never wanted to be without them.

"You've noticed the sighing?" Emma questioned.

Nora and Jackson nodded in unity. Nora reached her hand across the table and placed it gently on top of Emma's hand.

"We're worried about you, Emma. We just want you to be our happy little girl," Nora spoke gently and stroked her hand.

"That's just the problem," Emma finally said while holding back the tears building up inside her. "How long is that going to last? You will see that you don't need me anymore, and then I'll be alone again. Maybe once I'm finished with the kitchen, that will be the end of it. You'll have your new kitchen, and I'll have to return to my life without any reason to see you guys again." The tears were too strong to hold back, and they began to pour down her cheeks.

"I'm probably going to finish the kitchen this week, and then what? Are you still going to want me around? Do you think either of you will make the hour drive down to the city to see me? No, you won't! And I don't blame you for it. I'm used to people leaving me in my life, and I'm used to being alone. I understand why people don't want me around, and I understand that once the kitchen is finished, this will all be over. I just don't want to get too attached before that day comes," Emma explained.

Emma gently pulled her hand free of Nora's and picked the menu back up. She stared down at it blankly, not seeing what was on it but using it to avoid looking at Jackson and Nora. They both shared a look, and Jackson shook his head slightly. He knew that it would take some convincing from their part to put Emma's fears at ease.

Chapter 7

The house was gloomy, with the only noise coming from the kitchen and echoing through the house. Emma was hard at work. It was the end of the workweek, and the cupboards and benchtops were installed. Next was installing the appliances and then the tiling. Jackson had locked himself in his study, as usual, but he couldn't get any work done. It had nothing to do with the distraction of the noise. He couldn't concentrate because all he could think about was Emma leaving once the kitchen was finished. They would be gaining the best kitchen money could buy, but they would be losing something far greater. Nora felt the same way, knowing that no matter how much she loved her new kitchen, she loved having Emma as her little more.

He knew he needed to do something about it and stop Emma leaving. If she left, he would never forgive himself for letting it happen. He couldn't decide this on his own. Unlike most business decisions, Nora let him make without her this decision required both of them.

Jackson locked the room and searched through the house for Nora. She wasn't in their bedroom doing her makeup, and she wasn't working in her study. He checked downstairs, being careful not to be spotted by Emma. She was busy in the kitchen, but Nora was nowhere to be seen. Jackson thought she might be out in the garden, but he decided that if she were feeling the same way he was, she would be in her art room. She usually went there when she was upset or trying to distract herself.

Jackson made his way straight there. Just as he thought she had her music on full blast, she redirected her emotions into her art. She often wore old, torn up clothes, so she didn't mind getting paint on them. Jackson walked in as she danced around the room, splattering paint all over a blank canvas. She never painted anything specific. She would open up multiple cans of paint, all different colors, and dipped her big brush in before whipping it at the canvas in all directions to create splatters of paint.

Jackson loved to watch her, but he had no time to do so now. He needed to discuss something very important. He walked straight towards her stereo and turned down the music. Nora stopped in place the moment the music stopped and looked towards Jackson.

"Is something wrong?" Nora asked as she put her brush down.

"Was the music too loud?" She asked.

"No, I can't hear your music while I'm in my study, but that's not why I'm here," Jackson informed her. "I'm here because we need to talk about Emma."

"I know we do, but there's not much we can do. She's made her choice," Nora sighed and collapsed in her chair.

"She hasn't made her choice. She only thinks she has because she thinks we have made a choice, but we haven't yet. Have we?" Jackson asked.

Nora raised her eyebrow, "I'm not sure I follow."

"Emma doesn't believe that we want her to stay around after she's finished with the kitchen. We need to convince her that simply isn't true. It isn't true, is it?" Jackson questioned, clarifying his meaning.

"No, it's not. I want her to stay. I love having her around, and I love having her as our little," Nora let out another sigh. "I'm afraid I've begun sighing more often than Emma."

"If we want her as our little, for more than just a few dates, then we should tell her," Jackson stated. He walked towards Nora and placed his hands on her shoulders.

"I think we should tell Emma that we want her as our little. Not just as a play partner, but as exclusive little who we support, and that we want her to be with us," Jackson adamantly said.

"Really?" Nora said as she jumped out of the chair. "You want her to stay? Stay here with us and be our little permanently?"

Jackson nodded his head, "I think that would be the best solution for all of us."

"Yes! Yes, Jackson, I want that so much. I want her to be our little and stay here with us. Let's tell her, please!" Nora was more excited about the decision

"Not now," Jackson insisted.

"After she's finished the kitchen today. We'll take her out for dinner once it's done and ask her then. I am sure she'll say yes, but just be prepared that she might say no. Alright?" Jackson said, not wanting to get Nora's hopes up just to have her heart shattered. Nora danced around the room, quietly cheering as Jackson watched her. The noise from the kitchen filled the house once again, and they patiently counted down the days for Emma to finish.

The days past, the weekend coming and going with Emma having to face the reality that Monday had arrived. She had finally finished the kitchen. She'd been putting off thinking about it the whole weekend, knowing it might be the last weekend she gets to be Nora and Jackson's little. She knew that they asked her to be their little during play scenes and enjoying the DDLG and MDLG dynamic with them when she wasn't working, and that meant something, but she just didn't see how it could continue when she lived so far away. Now that she had finished the kitchen, there will be no reason to drive out here. She also won't have much time to do so, even if you wanted to.

Emma faced the ugly truth and got straight to work Monday morning. She tightened a few bolts, clean up a few loose ends, and make sure everything is in place. Nora and Jackson left her alone to do her job. They knew this was an important and challenging day for her, so they didn't want to distract her or get in her way. However, when she was finished, they were ready and waiting for her in the living room.

"All done!" Emma announced as she joined them. She was dirty and sweaty, but that was to be expected. "Do you want to have a look at your new kitchen?" She asked.

Nora was the first off the couch, followed by Jackson. Emma walked behind them and held her breath, waiting for their reaction. Nora gasped as her eyes set sight on the new kitchen that she and Emma had specially designed.

"This is wonderful," each word came out of Nora's mouth slowly and with effort. She was so in awe that she barely had the words to explain.

She danced around the large open room towards the windows on the opposite end. The sunlight from outside shone and lit up the room, making it look even more luxurious.

The appliances were silver and spotless. They glowed under the sunlight and added a fresh, new look to the kitchen. Emma watched Nora glide around the room as if she was floating on the clouds in the sky. She glanced up at Jackson now and again to try and gauge his reaction, but he was as hard as a stone as usual.

Finally, Emma grew tired of waiting for Jackson to speak, so she asked, "What do you think?" Her question wasn't directed at him, but she hoped he would answer along with Nora.

"It's amazing, Emma!" Nora replied straight away, squealing, and dancing in a circle. "I'm going to spend all day and night in this kitchen. I'm going to cook breakfast, lunch, dinner, dessert, and everything in between. I'm going to have all the parties in the world and invite everyone over because they can all fit in here now. It's the best, Emma!" Nora exclaimed. Emma was glad to hear how much Nora liked the kitchen, but she knew that Nora would. She needed to hear Jackson's thoughts because she could never tell what he was thinking behind his still, emotionless features. She wanted his approval. She needed it. She stared at him, hoping he'll say something.

"It's great," he finally spoke softly and calmly, but with a grin on his face and pride in his eyes. "You did a great job, Emma. No one could have done it better."

Emma let out a sigh of relief. A weight lifted off of her chest, and she couldn't be more proud of herself. She knew that Nora would love whatever she did, but she was stunned that she could impress Jackson. That was all that she could hope for.

"Jackson," Nora sang as she skipped across the kitchen and wrapped her arms around his neck. "Should we tell her now?"

Emma squinted at them as Jackson looked down at Nora.

"I don't see why not," Jackson responded.

"Emma, Nora, and I would like to ask you something," Jackson told her.

Emma took a step back, and her brow furrowed. She couldn't imagine what they would ask her, and her mind went wild thinking of what it could be.

"We want you to come out to dinner with us tonight," Nora said. "It's a date. You can quickly shower if you'd like and change into an outfit from my wardrobe if you don't have anything you'd like to wear."

"Really?" Emma stepped towards them once again as she thought about it. The only thing waiting for her at home was a microwave dinner and a romantic comedy. "Okay, that sounds like fun!" Emma replied, knowing that Nora's wardrobe was filled with lovely clothes. Emma showered and changed, and then they headed out for dinner. It was odd that Nora and Jackson had asked her out so suddenly, but Emma knew that they wanted to make the most of their short time together, so she didn't question it. Emma wasn't sure where they were going. It was a surprise.

Emma felt like a kid again, sitting in the back seat nervously, waiting for whatever was waiting for her at the end of the drive. They took a few back roads, and Emma knew that she would be lost if she was by herself. They were so far out in the countryside that there were no streetlights to light their way. It was pitch black wilderness around them aside from the car's headlights. Emma felt a mixture of fear and excitement, but her need to see where they were going outweighed her emotions. After the long drive, lights finally appeared in front of them. They were dim but easy to see in the dark. Jackson drove straight towards them. As they grew closer to the lights, an old, small cabin appeared in front of them. It was half made of wood and half made of stone. It was old and quaint. Emma imagined it had been sitting here for years, yet there were lights on and life moving inside. The windows were open, allowing the country music to spill out into the night air. There were a few cars and motorbikes parked outside, but there was one space left. He parked, and they both got out. Emma waited patiently for Jackson to let her out.

He opened the door just wide enough to stick his head inside, "Are you going to be a good girl tonight?"

"This place has the best brownie dessert!"

Nora cheered behind him.

"If you're a good girl, then we'll get you your bowl of ice-cream and a plate of brownies for dessert," Jackson added. Emma beamed up at them and nodded her head. She'll play along, for just one more night, before it's all over. Jackson let her out of the car, and Nora grabbed her hand. They led her up the creaky wooden stairs and into the building.

Inside was ripe with the smell of beer and burgers. Emma liked it. It reminded her of the pubs she used to visit with the guys when they weren't busy getting too drunk. There weren't a lot of people inside, but the few customers looked content. They all seemed to know each other, and they all seemed to know Nora and Jackson.

"Hey, Jackson! You're back for another round of pool!" One of the men called from the other end of the room.

"Not tonight, Jasper, I'm just here to have dinner," Jackson replied.

They carried on walking to the far side of the room where an empty table by an open window was waiting for them. Jackson pulled Emma's seat out and waited for her to sit down. He pushed her chair in, and he sat down between her and Nora.

"You don't need to look at the menu, dear," Nora told Emma. "Daddy's going to order for you." Emma liked the lack of control. She trusted Jackson and Nora to take control of her meal and order her the things she wanted and liked. This was everything she ever wanted in her life, and it was everything that she had been missing until she had met Nora and Jackson. A man entered the cabin and waved to Jackson and Nora the moment he spotted them. Emma noticed how most of the people in the room seemed to look at Nora and Jackson as if they knew them.

"Do you guys come here a lot?" She asked them.

"All the time. We love it here," Nora told

her. "Jackson owns it. He inherited from his father. This place is amazing. So down to earth and natural, you know?"

Emma smirked at the way Nora talked about the restaurant. She was filled with passion. She acted as though this place was their home, and they've lived here their whole lives.

"My father always loved good old fashioned country atmosphere like this," Jackson explained. "But he could never bring himself to move out here and live in the country. My mother never cared for the countryside that much, and he couldn't leave her behind for his dream. Instead, he decided to make this place a sort of home away from home. I admired his vision."

"Wow, that sounds so amazing," Emma gasped.

Jackson ordered burgers for the table, and Emma allowed them to take full control of the evening. She was the little after all, and they were her Mommy and Daddy. Allowing them to take control made it so much easier for her to relax and enjoy the night.

The waitress, dressed in a pretty plaid dress with her hair in a braid, brought them their burgers and drinks. Emma took one bite of the burger, and she was in heaven. The juicy, meaty taste swam down her throat, and she wanted more. Her fingers were covered in the burger's juices while she ate. It was the best burger she had ever eaten.

Nora giggled, grabbed a tissue from her bag, and leaned over the table. She gently wiped the sauce off of Emma's face and fingers before she continued eating.

"Remember to drink while you eat, sweetheart, or you'll get a terrible tummy-ache," Nora advised her.

"Don't make too much of a mess, or there'll be no dessert," Jackson warned her gently. He gave her a wink, so she didn't take it too seriously.

Emma widely grinned before she continued to

dig into the burger. The night had only just begun, and she couldn't see how it could get any better.

"Emma, before we eat dessert, Nora and I want to ask you something," Jackson said, changing his tone to be soft and serious.

"We discussed it earlier today, and we're both in agreement," he looked to Nora. She gave him a nod of approval. "Nora and I love having you around, and, if you want, we would like you to be our little, for more than just some dynamic and power play. Like, as a constant, ours and ours alone, little," Jackson explained. Emma's mouth dropped open, and her hands went limp. She nearly dropped the other half of the burger on the table. It was too good to be true. She couldn't fathom that someone would actually want her to be their little, and now two people wanted her. It was her dream come true. Something that she had only fantasized about, and yet she was sure that she heard Jackson say they wanted her.

"Are you serious?" Emma quietly asked as if she couldn't ask the question too loudly, or it might only be a dream.

"Yes, we're serious, Emma," Jackson continued. "If you want us as your Mommy and Daddy, we want you to be our little. There will be rules, and if you break those rules, there will be punishments-"

"But if you're a good girl, there'll be rewards to show that we are proud of you," Nora interrupted. "That's if you want to be ours." Emma didn't have to think about it, and she didn't hesitate for a moment. She knew exactly what she wanted, and it had nothing to do with going back to her small, empty apartment and being alone again.

"Yes," Emma said the instant Jackson and Nora were finished speaking. "Yes, I want to be your little, and I want you to be my Mommy and Daddy,"

Emma's cheeks hurt from how wide she was smiling, but she couldn't help herself. She was nearly jumping out of her seat and dancing around the room, but she contained herself. She wouldn't be a good girl if she caused a scene.

"We can discuss the rules, punishments, and rewards over dessert," Jackson suggested, wearing a smile almost as wide as Emma's, but still managing to keep his calm exterior. "Now, finish up your dinner, young lady." Emma nodded and ate her burger a bit slower and neater. She liked that Jackson was stern with her but not too much. They were the perfect mix of discipline and love.

Just as Jackson promised, they received their desserts and started discussing the rules. Emma got a bowl of ice-cream and a plate of brownies, just like Nora said she would. Emma agreed with some of the rules and added a few of her own. When they started discussing the rewards and punishments, she was very involved. She wanted to make sure none of the punishments were too much and that all of the rewards were worth it. When they finished, they ordered a few drinks and stayed for a while. Nora and Emma danced on the dance floor while Jackson watched. He changed the music in the jukebox so something slower and joined Nora on the dance floor. Emma sat back and watched them dance. She smiled, perfectly content with her life at this exact moment. Everything was perfect.

***

Jackson searched for his keys and struggled to open the door. Emma had her arms wrapped around his neck as his broad shoulders carried her from the car into the house. She wasn't tired. She just wanted him to carry her. Nora turned the lights on as they walked into the house and closed the door behind them.

"Do you want us to tuck you into bed?" Nora asked Emma.

"I'm not tired!" Emma complained. "I want to stay up a little longer."

"That's against the rules, Emma," Jackson

explained. "You know it's past your bedtime."

"Can't that start tomorrow? I've been a good girl all night," Emma said, looking up at them with her big pleading eyes.

"She's got a good point," Nora agreed. "I think we can let her stay up just a little longer."

"Okay, but if you're not tired, then I don't need to carry you anymore,"
Jackson put Emma down gently, and Nora went into the kitchen to make some tea. They set up some of the kitchen appliances on the few counters that Emma managed to install, so the kitchen was half usable.
Emma and Jackson sat down in the living room while Nora made the tea. Emma sat on the floor with the coloring book Nora bought her while Jackson turned on some soothing jazz music for himself. When Nora brought in the tea, they all sat around the coffee table and drank together, while the music played in the background.
After a while, Nora dimmed the lights, making it hard for Emma to see her coloring book.

"I think this type of playtime is over, baby girl," Nora said as she sat down next to Emma. "Don't you agree, Daddy?"

"Yes, I do. I think another playtime is about to start."

Nora inched forward and leaned into Emma. She breathed in Emma's ear as she ran the tips of her fingers up the center of her chest. She played with the zipper on Emma's hoodie and slowly pulled it down so her breasts would pop out. Emma was never sure what to do in these situations, but she was sure that she would tell her if they wanted her to do anything.

"Do you want to watch?" Nora asked Jackson.

Jackson didn't speak. He nodded his head slightly as he undid his pants.

Nora placed her hand on Emma's chest and gently pushed her down to the ground. They lay next to each other, and Nora began to kiss her neck.

"Unbutton my blouse," Nora demanded in

a whisper.

Emma did as she was instructed and undid the buttons on Nora's blouse. Nora's breasts becoming exposed as each button came undone.

"Play with them," Nora told her. Jackson watched as Emma played with Nora's breasts while she moved her lips from Emma's neck to her lips. She stuck her tongue through Emma's lips, and it danced in her mouth. Jackson stuck his hand down his pants and rubbed himself. His cock grew in his pants, and he groaned softly. Nora moved her hand down Emma's body and pushed it down her pants. Emma gasped as she felt Nora's fingers push against her clit gently. She swirled them around in a circle making Emma moan. Emma grew wetter. The more Nora played with her.

"Take off your pants, sweetie," Nora demanded.

Emma struggled to push her pants down as Nora continued to play with her gently. Nora pulled her hand away from Emma's clit only to undress her further. She pulled her hoodie and shirt off, leaving Emma lying naked on the floor. Nora pushed Emma's legs open and pressed her mouth against her pussy. Nora's tongue swirled around her clit, and Emma cried out. She glanced over at Jackson as he growled softly on the couch. His legs shook, and his body quivered as he continued to rub up and down. He stared at them intensely, wanting to be inside one of them. Nora reached down and began to play with herself as she stuck her small tongue inside of Emma. Emma let out a gasp as the new sensation tickled up and down her spine. She arched her back and pushed her pussy into Nora's mouth.

Jackson growled louder as he couldn't take it anymore. He pushed himself off the couch and joined them on the floor. He moved Nora aside gently as he pushed himself deep inside of Emma. Nora got up on her knees and pressed her breasts against his chest. They wildly kissed as Jackson stuck his fingers inside of her. He pumped up and down into Emma as he pushed his whole hand inside Nora.

"Yes! Yes!" Nora moaned as she dug her nails into his back.

Jackson groaned, and Emma felt his cock twitch inside of her. The ecstasy built up even more, and she knew she was ready to explode. She arched her back more, helping Jackson push his cock even further inside of her. She moaned louder and louder, and she was just about to scream when the soft jazz music was interrupted by the ringing of a phone.

Chapter 8

Nora cursed under her breath and jumped up. She buttoned the bottom of her blouse and tousled her hair as she raced across the room for her phone. Nora answered the phone and disappeared into the other room for a while. Jackson handed Emma a blanket so she wouldn't get too cold while they were waiting.

"I'm so sorry," Nora said as she came back into the room. "I have to go down to the office. There's an emergency with the final cut of that film we just finished, and it's due to be released soon. If we don't sort it out tonight, we'll have to push our release date back, and the company isn't going to like that."

"Do you need my help?" Jackson asked her coming to rest on his elbows.

Nora fixed her clothes and touched up her hair and makeup faster than Emma had ever seen anyone do it before. She looked as though she was ready to go to a business meeting within seconds.

"No, I'll be fine. You stay here with Emma, and I'll try to get back as soon as I can," Nora grabbed her bag and kissed Emma on the cheek.

"Goodbye, sweetie, Daddy is going to take good care of you while I'm away," Nora hugged and kissed Jackson goodbye before passing her the keys, and she disappeared out the front door. Jackson didn't waste any time coming back to Emma. He placed his one hand by the small of her back and looped the other arm under her knees. He lifted her off the floor and carried her up the stairs.

"I'm going to take good care of you, Emma, so just close your eyes and relax," Jackson whispered.

"Thank you, Daddy," Emma sighed, relaxing into his strong arms.
He took her to the bathroom and gently placed her in the bath. He ran some hot water and poured in plenty of rose-scented bubble bath. Emma leaned back as the hot water surrounded

her and warmed her from the inside out. Jackson grabbed a cloth and soaked it in the water. He ran it up and down her back gently, scrubbing away the scent of beer and sweat from the night. He grabbed her head and gently lowered it into the water, taking the cloth and wiping her face. Emma allowed her body to go limp as Jackson cared for her. He paid extra attention to her hands and feet while she lay back.

When she was clean, he lifted her out of the bath and rubbed her dry with a soft, fluffy towel. He wrapped the towel around her and carried her to the guest bedroom. He laid her down and began to diaper her, pulling the tabs tight before putting her in a onesie and cuddling with her as she fell asleep, sucking her thumb.

***

Emma hadn't even noticed she was falling asleep or when Jackson left to let her sleep in the room alone. She woke up when she heard Nora turn off the shower. Emma hopped out of bed and got ready. She was grateful that most of Nora's clothes fit her, so she didn't have to worry about wearing her work clothes.

Emma had just finished making her bed when the door slowly opened, and Nora peeked her head inside.

"Good, you're awake. Oh, baby girl, and you've already made your bed!" Nora smiled proudly at her. "You're such a good girl. Come downstairs, and I'll make you some breakfast." Nora closed the door behind her, and Emma heard her footsteps fade down the stairs. Emma was ready to follow after her, but she didn't want to seem too eager. This was her first full day as their little, and she wasn't sure how she was supposed to act. She waited a few minutes before going downstairs to meet them.

Nora was in the kitchen, making toast and tea. Emma looked around, but Jackson wasn't there.

"I was thinking, since you were so good

yesterday and I had to leave last night, I would treat you to a little outing today," Nora suggested as Emma walked into the room. "Jackson has gone to the office to make sure everything was done correctly last night, so I thought it might be nice to have some Mommy, baby time. We can do whatever we want!" Nora said as she poured Emma some tea and buttered the toast.

"That sounds great," Emma agreed. "What do you want to do, Mommy?" Emma asked. She loved being able to call Nora and Jackson Mommy and Daddy. It made her feel as though everything was finally going to be alright.

"It's a surprise," Nora teased as she carried their breakfast into the sitting room with Emma following close behind. "Jackson took his car, so we'll have to use mine, but you get to sit in the front with me," Nora explained.

"Yay!" Emma cheered as she sat down for breakfast.

They ate their breakfast and left the house straight away. Emma put her seatbelt on in the front seat of the car with Nora, Nora pulling on it to double-check it was tight enough.

"Do you remember the rules?" Nora asked as they drove away from the house.

"Yes, Mommy, I remember," Emma informed her. "I can't wander off or stray too far. I must be in your sight at all times. If I want something, I have to ask for it nicely and not whine if you say 'no.' I have to eat all my food, and I'm not allowed junk food or soda."

"That's okay, you don't have to list all of them," Nora lovingly laughed, as she interrupted her. "I just wanted to make sure you still remember what we discussed last night. If you follow all the rules today, I'll buy you a special toy!"

Emma jumped up and down in her seat to show her excitement. They drove into the city where Emma lived, but they didn't go anywhere near her apartment or office. They went into the part of the city that Emma rarely visited, the fancier part.

Nora took Emma to all sorts of places, and they did a lot of Mommy, little activities. They went to a salon first and got their hair done. Emma let Nora control what the hairdresser did to her hair. They trimmed it slightly, then washed and styled it. After that, they visited a few clothing shops, and Nora spoiled Emma with bags full of new clothes because she was good at the salon when Nora had taken over 3 hours to get her hair done.

They stopped at a coffee shop and chatted over tea and donuts. Emma spilled her tea a little and made a mess with her donuts, but Nora didn't scold her. She cleaned up, and they left. They drove around for a while, looking for a place to eat lunch, singing along to the songs on the radio. When they found a place to eat, they sat there for a while until Nora ordered for both of them.

"We shouldn't stay out too long," Nora said as she glanced at her watch. "Daddy will start to wonder where we are. You were such a good girl today, Emma. You made Mommy very proud. We've about an hour before we need to leave. Mommy is going to let you choose what we do."

"Whatever I want, Mommy?" Emma felt overwhelmed with the power and the possibilities of her choice, but she was also excited.

She thought about what she wanted to do before they went home while finishing her lunch. There were a lot of things they could do, but she didn't want to choose anything that would take too long. She knew Jackson would be waiting for them. She wanted to do something fun and short with Nora.

Emma gazed out of the window and noticed an ice-cream truck sitting on the opposite side of the road, next to a small park. That was the exact moment that Emma knew what she wanted to do.

They left the restaurant and crossed the street to the ice-cream truck. Nora ordered them both a waffle-cone, with chocolate ice-cream and nut sprinkles. They then made their way to the park and sat on the swings while they ate their ice-cream. Emma couldn't stop smiling. She felt so warm inside as she shared this simple, small moment with Nora.

***

"Emma, Jackson, and I were discussing something very important last night while you were asleep," Nora explained the following day as Emma sat at the kitchen bench. Nora had made her breakfast, and Jackson was reading the newspaper on his tablet as he sipped his coffee.

"You live near the center of the city, and although we travel there often for our work, it is still an hour away," Jackson continued. "It just doesn't make sense for you to be our little and live out there." Emma's heart dropped to the pit of her stomach as her mind ran wild with what Jackson was about to tell her. She knew this day would come at some point, that they would say they wanted her just for them to change their minds. Emma was used to good things ending. It was the way of life as far as she knew it.

"We want you to move in with us, Emma," the words floated out of Nora's mouth, and with her silky voice, it sounded like a dream to her. Emma looked up slowly and studied their faces. They weren't joking or messing with her. The words they spoke were genuine. She couldn't believe that this was happening to her.

"You want me to move in?" Emma asked, her mind still catching up with the words that her ears heard. "You want me to move into this house with you?" Nora nodded, and Jackson gave a slight smile.

"Yes!" Emma exclaimed. "Yes, I want to move in with you. I'll have to pack my stuff, sell the big stuff I can't bring, and I'll have to give notice to my landlord, but I want to move in."

"Perfect!" Nora jumped up. "Don't worry about all that technical stuff, baby. Daddy is good with that sort of thing. You don't have to sell any of your things. We can put them in storage, just in case."

"Today, why don't we drive you there, and you can pack some of your clothes and essentials to bring here in the meantime," Jackson suggested.

"Yes, Daddy," Emma agreed, the smile on her face melting Nora and Jackson's hearts.

Chapter 9

Jackson and Nora followed Emma in their car to Emma's apartment. When they got there, Jackson parked out on the street in front of her building, took his seatbelt off, and leaned into the back seat.

"Do you want me to come up and help you pack little one?" He asked her.

"That's okay, Daddy. It's only a few things. I'll be quick," Emma assured him. "I'm just going to pack a few days' worth of clothes, toothbrush, and stuff."

"Don't forget your paci. We'll wait here then, just call for us if you need help with anything, sweetheart," Nora told her as she opened the door.

Emma rushed through the doors of her building and ran up the stairs. She took the steps two at a time. If she could fly up to them, she would. This was the best night of her life, and she couldn't wait to drag her bags through the doors of Nora's and Jackson's house and call it her own.

She looked down at her feet to make sure she wouldn't miss a step or trip. When she looked back up, a man was in her way, and her shoulder slammed into his. She stumbled forward and darted to the side, holding her shoulder in pain.

"Sorry about that," she cried at the guy as she continued up the stairs.

Nothing was going to stop her or slow her down. She looked over her shoulder just before she disappeared around the corner and further up the stairs. She noticed that she only ran into one of the men, but there were four of them altogether. She didn't recognize their faces from around the building, but then again, she didn't spend a lot of time socializing with her neighbors. She pushed their faces out of her mind and continued on her way to her apartment.

She got to the third floor and pushed the keys into the lock of her door. She threw it open and started packing immediately. She grabbed a backpack from under her bed and rushed to the window. Nora and Jackson's car still sat at the corner of the street in front of her building. She didn't want to keep them waiting too long. Emma grabbed some clothes from her closet and threw them in the bag on the bed. She rushed into the bathroom, grabbed her toothbrush, hairbrush, shampoo, her box of little things, and her perfume. She walked back into the living area and headed for the couch when she froze, mouth open, eyes wide, and stared at the dark figure standing by her front door.

Her arms went limp, and the things she was carrying crashed to the floor. She glanced at the window and thought of running to it and calling for Jackson and Nora down below. The figure moved into the apartment towards her, and three more figures moved in through the door behind him.

Emma had forgotten to turn the lights on, just how she had forgotten to close and lock the door behind her. The first figure stepped in front of the window, and the setting sun's light fell on his face. The face of the man she ran into on the stairs grinned at her.

"Well, aren't you a pretty little thing," the man spoke in a greedy voice.
Emma swallowed hard, but the lump in her throat grew stronger, stopping her from breathing or calling for help. Her eyes glanced around the room, looking for some kind of escape or way of protecting herself, but she had nothing. She was trapped. The men closed in, surrounding her and making any movement impossible.
The last man to enter the apartment and slammed the door behind him, and Emma knew there was no one around to help her now. Jackson and Nora were so close and yet so far away. She forced herself to look into the eyes of the man walking towards her.

"You know, it was kind of rude how you ran into me on the stairs earlier," he spoke slowly as he pulled a black pocket knife from his jacket pocket. "Since you're so pretty, I'll forgive you, but you've got to give me something in return." He pressed into Emma's body and placed the cold steel of the knife against her cheek. He leaned forward and whispered in her ear, "What are you willing to do for my forgiveness?" Emma wanted to collapse to the floor and burst into tears, but she refused to appear weak in front of this man. The other three men walked closer and giggled as he moved the point of the knife down towards her breast. He pierced her top with the knife and sliced it open, revealing just a hint of her cleavage.

That was it. Emma's face grew hard, and she threw her hands out in front of her. She pushed the guy away from her and made a break for it. She rushed towards the front door, but one of the men grabbed her arm and pulled her back. Her body was so small and light that they threw her up against the wall next to the window. She crashed into a table on the way down, knocking over a glass vase that smashed on the floor.

The man with the knife got to his feet and growled at Emma. She tried to push herself off the floor, but he mounted her before she had the chance. He held her one wrist to the ground with his free hand and placed his knee over her other wrist. Emma pushed, pulled, and struggled to free herself of his grip, but he was too strong for her.

He leaned forward, pressing his other knee into her ribs. She coughed and choked, but he didn't let up. He placed the knife against her neck and pressed his face up against hers, so she was forced to look into his eyes.

"I'll teach you some respect, girl," he spat at her. "I'll show you how you're supposed to treat a man. Women as pretty as you are made for one thing and one thing only, and that's exactly what you're going to give my boys and me tonight whether you like it or not."

He pressed the tip of the knife into her skin, and she cried out. She did her best to push him off of her, but he stood his ground. She kicked out, and he lost his footing. His hand slipped, and the knife cut deep across Emma's collarbone. She screamed as the cold steel pierced her skin, and her blood poured out of the wound onto the floor.

"Damn it bitch! Look what you made me do," the man yelled at her.

"That's enough, man," one of the other men stepped forward and pulled him off, Emma. "We weren't supposed to hurt her. We were just going to take some of her stuff and go." Emma took this as an opportunity to escape, but she didn't know where to go. She pushed herself up until she was sitting and crawled along the ground to the far corner of the room and sat with her back against the wall. The tears she'd been desperately trying to hold in began to pour down her face as she cradled her bleeding wound.

"You guys wanna chicken out?" The man screamed at them, throwing his knife around as a threat. "Go ahead! Get out of here! I'll have her myself then."

"Dude, give it a rest already," another one of the men stood up against him. "She ran into you on the stairs, so what? Let's just grab the cash and the stuff and get outta here before someone hears and calls the cops."

"Yeah, stealing is one thing, but I'm not game for whatever crazy train you're on," the third man agreed.

"You're all fucking weak!" The man with the knife spat at the ground at their feet. "You think you can call yourself men?"

"None of you can call yourself men," Jackson said, making Emma gasped as she heard the familiar, silky voice cut through the horror of the night.

The men turned to face the open doorway. They parted just enough for Emma to see Jackson standing in the doorway, towering over the men like a mountain. He stepped inside, and when his eyes fell on Emma in the corner, his face grew hard. He shot cold looks at the men.

"How dare you!" He growled at them,

bearing his teeth like an animal. "No man can claim to be a man if he is willing to raise his hand to a woman," Jackson said. Nora appeared behind Jackson in the hallway. Emma wanted to crawl to them. She wanted to crawl to safety, but the men stood in place.

"What's your problem, old man?" The man with the knife giggled as he walked towards Jackson. He held the knife out in front of him, pointing it directly at Jackson's chest.

"Why don't you and your old lady turn around and pretend you didn't see anything. If you don't, I'll kill you and have both of them for myself," the guy spat.

"You've made a big mistake," Jackson's tone was calm and emotionless.
The man with the knife laughed at Jackson while the other three began to slowly back away. They didn't know who this man was or what he was capable of, but he was big and looked strong. He towered over them, and his shoulders were almost wider than the doorway he just stepped

through. The man continued to laugh as Jackson walked towards him. He was too drunk from the power that the small knife gave him that he didn't expect Jackson to move as fast as he did. Jackson rushed across the room and grabbed the intruder's hand holding the knife. He pulled it towards him and wrapped his free hand around the man's wrist. Before he could react, Jackson twisted, and the sound of his wrist snapping echoed through the room, followed by the man's panicked screams. Jackson placed his palm against the man's chest and pushed him away. He flew across the room and slammed into the base of Emma's bed, hitting his head once on the corner of the bed, and a second time on the floor. The three remaining men looked down at their friend, who was ready to take all of them on, now unconscious on the floor, drooling from the corner of his mouth and wrist bent out. They looked back at Jackson, who was unharmed and without a single bead of sweat on his brow. Emma managed a smile through her tears of pain and fear. She knew that Jackson would protect her. She knew he would come running to rescue her. That's why she needed to fight. She needed to stay strong until he could find her and save her.

The men threw their hands up and back away from Jackson. They each begged him to let them go and not to hurt them. They insisted that none of this was their idea and that they weren't in on it. Jackson stayed silent, and his expression remained ice cold. He stood tall as he marched towards them, hands calm at his side.

Nora pushed into the apartment and rushed around the edge of the room towards Emma. She crouched down at Emma's side. The tears continued to pour as Nora cupped her hands around Emma's face. She held her close and comforted her as best she could while Jackson dealt with the rest.

The men continued to beg for mercy, but it seemed as though he wasn't willing to grant it. Jackson stepped forward, and one of the men

tried to make a break for it. He rushed towards
the open doorway, freedom within his grasp, but
Jackson grabbed his arm and pulled him back.
Jackson threw him against the wall, and he
slammed into the window, smashing his arm
through it.

The second man ran towards Jackson, hoping to
catch him off his guard, but Jackson turned to
face him and caught his fist in midair. Jackson
grabbed the man's hand and twisted his arm
behind his back, forcing his arm into the center
of his spine. The man cried out in pain and
begged Jackson to let go. Jackson continued to
twist his arm and push it into his back until a
loud popping sound could be heard. The man
screamed, and Jackson dropped him to the
ground. His arm was loose and limp by his side.

"You dislocated his shoulder!" The
remaining man cried out. "What the hell is
wrong with you?"

"You and your friends attacked a poor,
defenseless girl in her own home," Jackson

calmly spoke as if he did this sort of thing every day. "You deserve this."

"You're crazy," the man muttered and made a break for the door.
Jackson meant to follow him, but Nora's panicked, squeaky voice stopped him.

"Jackson!" she screamed at him. Jackson spun around, and his cold eyes fell on Nora's teary eyes. "Emma is hurt! She needs our help." Nora's voice was weak but demanding. Jackson stared at them for a while, unsure of what was happening or what he should think. He was angry, that much was obvious, but he was also scared. He was scared to think of what they could have done to Emma if they had not heard her scream from the street. If they were not here to defend her, what would have happened? Jackson's eyes grew soft, and a tear formed in the corner of one. It broke free and glided down his cheek as Jackson strode towards Emma and Nora. The blood still oozed from the wound on her collarbone. Jackson pulled off his jacket and wrapped it around Emma's arms to keep her warm. He then pulled off his shirt and placed it against the wound. He pressed gently, and Emma winced.

"Don't worry, sweetie, Mommy's got you," Nora whispered to her. "Should we take her to the hospital?"
Jackson thought for a moment and then nodded slightly, "We should call the police as well. Have them come and arrest these thugs." Jackson sighed and shook his head.

"You take Emma to the hospital, and I'll call the police. I'll stay here and deal with them in the meantime," he explained.
Nora nodded. Jackson lifted Emma and carried her down the stairs to the car waiting outside. He gently laid her down in the backseat and gave her a gentle kiss on the forehead before closing the door.

"I'll call you to let you know which hospital we're going to," Nora told Jackson as she climbed into the driver's seat. "Then you can tell the police where we are if they want our statements."

"Okay, drive safe," Jackson leaned through the window and kissed Nora.
Nora closed the window, turned the engine on, and drove away. Jackson remained in the street a while longer, watching them as they drove away. When the car's tail lights had disappeared, he went back up into Emma's apartment and proceeded to call the police. He wished that he could be in the car with Emma and Nora, and he wished that he could be the one carrying her into the hospital.

***

Emma's eyes flickered open, and she was blinded by the bright lights above her. The air around her was cold, and the walls were white. For a moment, she thought maybe she was in heaven, but the constant beeping of the machine by her side let her know that she was in a bed in a hospital room.

"How are you feeling?" Nora asked her. Emma looked at her with squinted eyes. She was sitting in a small chair beside Emma's bed. Her eyes slowly adjusted to the light in the room as she looked around, looking for Jackson. The rest of the room was empty. She looked back at Nora, who was now leaning forward and reaching for Emma's hand.

"Where's Jackson?" Emma asked, but her voice came out harsh and scratched her throat on the way. "He's probably still at your apartment. He needed to wait for the police. Those animals need to be locked up."

"I saw Jackson fighting, was that just a dream?" Emma softly asked.

The whole night became a blur for Emma. She felt the pain in her back from hitting the wall and the pain in her wrists from being pinned to the ground. She could still feel the pain on her collarbone from the cold knife, but the rest felt like a dream.

Did Jackson break that man's wrist and dislocate the other's shoulder? Did he throw someone through the window? Emma thought.

"He fought them off," Nora confirmed Emma's suspicions.

"Really," Emma couldn't believe that Jackson cared for her that much. "He wanted to fight those guys off for me. He wanted to protect me?"

"Of course he did, sweetie," Nora said, stroking Emma's forehead.

Nora reached across and laid her hand on top of Emma's hand. She stared into Emma's eyes for a few moments, but they were interrupted by the sound of Nora's ringtone. Nora cursed under her breath and quickly answered it. Emma thought she heard Jackson's voice on the other end, but she wasn't sure. Nora nodded to herself, agreed out loud, and hung up.

"The police are on their way," Nora informed Emma as she sat back down. "They probably just want to ask you a couple of questions to confirm that Jackson's story is true. Are you okay with that?"

Emma nodded. She would do anything if it meant helping Jackson. He saved her life, so it was the least that she could do. Nora seemed angry with him, but Emma couldn't understand why.

"When the police are finished, and the doctors say it's okay, then we'll take you home," Nora assured her. "Jackson and I can go back to your apartment, pack your things, or buy you new things. It doesn't matter. Mommy and Daddy are going to take you home, and we're going to take care of you. Would you like that?"

"Yes, Mommy," Emma's voice grew weak as she spoke, and her eyes started to close. "I want to go home."

Chapter 10

Emma spent a few days in the hospital, as the doctors said that the cut was deep and required stitches. They also kept her in for monitoring as she showed signs of deteriorating mental health. Once Emma was ready to go home, Nora and Jackson were ready and waiting to take her. They had already moved most of her things out of her apartment while she had been lying in her hospital bed. They packed all her clothes and moved them into the house, and they moved most of her furniture into a storage unit. Jackson and Nora handled everything, so Emma didn't have to.

Jackson dealt with the police and the thugs, so Emma didn't need to see their faces again. She answered a few questions for the police, and they never bothered her again. Emma was grateful to have someone like Jackson to handle the situation. He knew what he was doing, and nothing seemed to faze him.

Nora grabbed Emma's things while Jackson helped put on her shoes. He gave her his arm, and she leaned on it while they walked out of the hospital. Jackson helped her walk to the car and into the back seat. They drove home, and she said goodbye to the hospital, hoping never to see it again.

Emma didn't think she would feel so free while driving away from the city. They left the highway and entered the dirt roads of the countryside. Emma leaned against the window and watched the wildlife fly by. They were on their way to her new home.

Emma spent the next few days lying lifeless in her bed while Nora and Jackson nursed her back to health. Her stitches needed cleaning once a day, and her bandages needed to be changed. Emma felt limp. She couldn't move, and she didn't have the motivation or energy to do anything.

Nora and Jackson did their best to make her comfortable, but she just felt like giving up. She was weak, and she knew it. She couldn't even protect herself from a couple of punk kids. She was stupid enough to leave the door wide open, practically inviting them in. Emma felt as though she wasn't worthy of the attention she was getting from Jackson and Nora. She put them in danger, and she wasn't worthy of being their little.

Every day since she returned from the hospital was the same. Nora walked into her room early in the morning and opened up all the curtains and windows so that some light and air could flood the room. She would then check if Emma was willing to get up and come downstairs for breakfast. Emma would just lie there and not say a word. Most days, she would keep her eyes closed and pretend to be still asleep.

Nora would bring her up some breakfast, usually toast or cereal, with some tea, but Emma wouldn't eat it alone. Nora was more than happy to sit Emma up and feed her. Emma hated that she was going through so much effort to care for her, but she couldn't find the strength to do it herself.

Emma would lie in bed for the rest of the morning until Jackson came back from work. Jackson would visit Emma around the same time each day. He would lift her out of her bed and place her in a chair by the window. Then he would sit with her and read a book to her. He would ask her to pick a book, but if she didn't respond, he would choose one anyway.

Jackson liked to sit in the sun by the window with her. He thought that she needed it in her life, and so did he. They would sit there for hours at a time until Nora came to feed her lunch. Jackson would sometimes help; other times, he would go to his study to finish up some work. Later in the day, Jackson would carry Emma to the bathroom, undress her, and draw a nice hot bath. He added plenty of bubble bath and used a nice body wash when he cleaned her. He brought a new body wash to try every day, and he would always ask her if she liked the smell. Emma never responded. She hadn't said more than a few words to either of them since they brought her back from the hospital.

For dinner time, Jackson would carry Emma downstairs, and they would all sit together in the sitting room. Nora enjoyed cooking in her new kitchen, and she made a new dish every night. Emma still refused to feed herself, but Jackson was there to help Nora feed her at dinner time. To end the day, Jackson carried Emma to the living room, and they all sat and watched a movie. They would ask Emma which movie she wanted to watch, but she never answered. Sometimes they would try to play Monopoly, but she would just sit and let Nora roll the dice for her. Emma was always carried up the stairs and tucked into bed before ten. They wanted her to get lots of rest. Nora would tuck her in and give her an extra duvet on cold nights, and then both she and Jackson would give her a kiss goodnight. Some nights Jackson would read her to sleep. She liked listening to his smooth, deep voice. It relaxed her, but the empty feeling never left, no matter what.

This was how Emma's days went, and Nora and Jackson tried their best to get their little girl back to the way she used to be.

***

Jackson met Nora at the hospital after work. She waited for him at the reception desk, and when their name was called, they walked straight into the doctor's office.

"How can I help you today?" The doctor asked them. "Is Emma not with you?"

"No, doctor, that's the problem," Nora explained. "We can barely get her to leave her bed. She does nothing. She's completely shut down, and we don't know what to do."

The doctor nodded her head and sighed. She sat down behind her desk and thought of the best way to explain to Jackson and Nora what was going on.

"I'm afraid this can sometimes happen," she started. "She underwent a traumatic experience, and for most people, a life or death experience like that can change you. Everyone reacts differently. Emma's reaction to the situation is just one of many."

"You're telling us that what she's doing is normal?" Jackson asked as his brows furrowed.

"It's a normal and expected reaction, yes, but it is also an unhealthy one in the long run. If someone were to shut down completely, as Emma has done, it's quite possible that they can stay in that state for a long time," the doctor explained.

"How can we help her, doctor?" Nora leaned forward in her chair. "Please, there must be something we can do. Maybe there is some kind of medicine, therapy, or something?"

"I wouldn't recommend giving Emma any kind of medicine at this stage," the doctor suggested while shaking her head. "Yes, you could probably use medication to wake her up a bit and give her more energy, but what Emma needs is a reason to wake up again. She's shut down for a reason. Now she needs an even better reason to snap out of it. I would suggest she sees a therapist as well."

Jackson nodded his head and laid a comforting hand on Nora's shoulder, "Thank you, doctor. We'll see what we can do."

Nora was silent the whole ride home. Jackson dared not break the silence. He knew how Nora felt. The ride home was short, but it felt like an eternity to Jackson. The moment they walked through the front door, Nora dropped her bag on the floor and headed straight to Emma's room. Jackson didn't join her. He picked up her bag and hung it up, then he wandered around the house, his mind running wild. He needed some way to save Emma. He needed to wake her up and give her a reason to rejoin their family. Jackson looked online for therapists in the area who specialized in trauma-related incidents, saving the details, and planning on sharing them with Emma.

Jackson walked into the kitchen and admired what Emma had done with it. Back when she first started, he was skeptical that she could do it all by herself, and he didn't believe that it would be worth the money he was spending on it. When Emma finished, he was stunned. He didn't say so at the time, but maybe he should have.

Jackson sat at the large table at the back of the room that Nora and Emma picked out. Every part of the kitchen was something that both Nora and Emma decided. Emma built this kitchen, but Nora poured her heart and soul into it.

Jackson remembered that day they ran around the old kitchen, making plans and drawing designs. He closed his eyes and recalled their faces when they brought their final design to him for approval. Their eyes were filled with hope and pure joy. Jackson wished he could see that look in their eyes one more time.

He sighed and pushed the memory out of his mind before it could make him feel any worse.

He walked up the stairs and thought of joining Nora and Emma in the room. He didn't want to lock himself in his study and pretend everything is okay.

He wandered about the house until he came to an empty room. He and Nora could never decide what to do with most of the rooms in the house. He always thought it was too big for them, but with Emma living there now, maybe it wouldn't seem as big anymore. Jackson smiled as an idea popped into his head. He knew how he could help Emma come back to life.

Jackson knocked on the door softly before he entered the room. Nora was sitting on a chair next to Emma's bed. Emma was sitting up in her bed, staring blankly ahead. He drew in a deep breath and walked into the room.

"I have an idea," he said. "Can you both come with me for a moment?"

Nora raised her eyebrow at him, but she didn't question it. She stood up, and Jackson lifted Emma out of bed. He carried Emma to the empty room, and Nora followed behind. He walked in and showed Emma around while Nora waited by the doorway, watching.

"What do you think?" He asked them.

"Of what," Nora sighed.

"Of Emma's new nursery," Jackson shot her a smug grin. "I figured she would need one if she is going to be living with us."
Nora pushed off the wall and walked further into the room. She looked around, seeing it in a new light this time.

"I guess this could do," Nora eventually said.

"Oh no, it won't do in this condition," Jackson told her. "It's just a boring empty room as it stands, but if you and Emma work together, you could design the perfect nursery together. Just like you two did to design the perfect kitchen." Jackson looked down at Emma limp in his arms.

"What do you think? Can you turn this boring, empty room into the best nursery ever imagined?" Nora asked.

Nora and Jackson stared at Emma, patiently waiting for her to say something or at least move. Emma remained still and silent for a while. Nora sighed and turned to leave the room, just as Emma lifted her head and looked around her.

"It is a boring room," Emma's voice was harsh and soft when she spoke, but hearing her speak brought a tear to Jackson's eye. "I can make it look better."

Nora spun around on her heels, and the tears began to flood down her cheeks. She looked at Jackson and then down at Emma. She ran towards them and threw her arms around them both.

"Then let's get started," Jackson whispered.

Emma's days changed drastically from that point. Emma and Nora both woke up early, and they spent most of their mornings looking over designs of nurseries and rooms on Nora's laptop.

They discussed what they both wanted for the room. Emma let Nora do most of the talking at first, but she would disagree or put forward her ideas now and again.

Jackson stayed out of their way most of the time, but sometimes he sat back and watched them work. He loved seeing the look in Emma's eye when she saw a room design that she loved and wanted to copy. Slowly Emma became more like herself. The addition of her therapy sessions helping her process the violent break-in.

Jackson and Nora were sitting in the bedroom. They hadn't started remodeling yet, but they had finalized their designs, and Nora was running Jackson through the changes they would make. Jackson listened carefully, but he didn't need to hear what Nora had to say. He was ready to approve any final design they had in mind. Emma knocked on the door and slowly walked into the room to join them. Jackson stood up immediately as she walked in. Emma smiled at both of them, and it was the first time they had seen her smile in weeks.

"What are you doing?" Emma asked them.

"I'm walking Jackson through your final design," Nora explained. Emma looked to Jackson with a glint in her eyes, "That's not Jackson, that's Daddy!" Jackson and Nora smiled, surprised that Emma was ready to move their dynamic back into their kink.

"What do you think, Daddy?" Emma asked as she came up onto the bed and snuggled into Jackson's lap.

"I love it," Jackson told her. "I think it's going to look amazing when you're done with it. It only matters if you like it, it's going to be your room, after all, baby girl."

"I know, but I want you to like it as well, Daddy," Emma replied, snuggling in close to him.

"Um, Daddy," Emma said, piquing Jackson's curiosity. Nora smiled, predicting what Emma was about to say and began to walk into her current bedroom.

"Can you put me in a diaper night, please?" Emma asked, wanting their dynamic to return. Jackson beamed down at her, raising his eyebrows, not wanting her to push herself too much.

"Are you sure that's something that you want, little one?" He questioned, whisking her up in his arms when she nodded yes.

"Well, alright, baby girl, let's get you into something a little more comfortable," he remarked, carrying her down the hallway to her room.

"Are you going to lay down for Daddy?" Jackson asked. Nora was already waiting in the room, holding a thick diaper in her hand and the baby powder in the other. Jackson undressed Emma and Nora opened up the diaper, Emma wriggling on top of it. Nora sprinkled the baby powder over Emma, rubbing it over Emma's body, bending down to kiss the tip of her nose.

"Keep your leggies down for me," Jackson

instructed as he fastened the diaper tabs around Emma's waist and began dressing her in her onesie. It had been a long time since Emma had been in a diaper, and she sucked her thumb as she watched Nora nad Jackson get her ready. She reached for them, making grabby hands as Jackson picked her up and settled her on his lap. Nora came to sit next to them on the bed, and Emma rested her head on Jackson's shoulder as her eyes became heavy.

"Sweet dreams, baby girl," Jackson said, kissing her cheek and holding her as she finally felt at peace.

Who is Tina Moore?

Tina Moore has enjoyed the lifestyle of a Mommy Domme for several years. She began secretly exploring kink and BDSM in her youth and found her love of being a strict Mommy Domme in early 2000. Tina Moore slowly became more comfortable and confident through making friends in the community and exploring the lifestyle and now openly celebrates being a Mommy Domme to her little.

Before becoming an author, Tina Moore worked in the finance sector, but it was through the encouragement of her current little that she took the leap and wrote her first MDLG book, Nancy's Little One.

From then on, Tina Moore continued to combine her experiences and desires, as well as the sweet and naughty things her baby girl does, to bring you tantalizing and salacious stories about both MDLG and DDLG relationships and the ABDL littles and middles who enjoy them.

Follow her on:

Author Page on Amazon

Instagram @tinamoore.kdp